The Tr

Chapter One

A crowd gathered on the grass behind Middle Falls High School. There was an opening in the middle of the crowd, and this is where two boys slowly circled each other. Their eyes never leaving one another's face, their fists moved slowly and rhythmically in front of them. One boy was tall and lean, the other a little shorter and stockier.

Stanley Dill, the taller of the two boys, let loose a powerful roundhouse. Ned Summers, the stockier boy, ducked and Stanley's fist connected with Ned's forehead.

Ned saw stars and fell to one knee. Meanwhile, Stanley broke his knuckle on Ned's hard head, although he didn't realize he'd done so for quite a while.

Down on one knee, Ned had the opportunity to do some real damage to Stanley's groin, but he didn't. This wasn't *that* kind of no-holds-barred fight. They were just outside Middle Falls High School, surrounded by a ring of other boys who were judging them—not just on whether they got beat, but *how* they fought.

Instead of the groin shot, Ned shook his head to clear the stars he was seeing. Then he drove his shoulder up into Stanley's solar plexus. The momentum of Ned's body knocked Stanley over backward and they ended up in a heap on the ground—the end result of almost every high school fight. Ned landed on top and got in one solid swipe to Stanley's face before Stanley was able to buck him off to the side. They rolled around and tussled for a few seconds before a meaty hand grabbed the back of Ned's collar and lifted him up, nearly choking him.

"That'll be enough."

The voice was calm but still carried the ring of authority. It was Mr. Temple, the principal. He wasn't a tall man, but he was built like a fireplug, and the boys attending Middle Falls High had long since decided it wasn't worth messing with him.

He let go of Ned, who again fell into a kneeling position on the grass.

Temple turned to the gathered crowd and said, "School's out for the day, boys. What are you still doing here? Would you like me to find something for you to do? I have a list and I'm happy to put you to work if you don't have somewhere else to be."

Ten seconds later, only Mr. Temple, Ned, and Stanley were left.

"That's the way it is with this generation. No one wants to pitch in and help," Temple said as he shrugged. He looked at Ned, who had no obvious injuries, aside from a red blotch on his forehead. Stanley looked like he'd gotten the worst of it. His nose was bleeding and his right eye already looked like a shiner might be in his future.

"Now... Why are you boys having at each other?"

Ned looked away, gazing at the horizon. That wasn't an easy question to answer.

A fight between Ned and Stanley had been inevitable for years. Nothing special happened to cause it today. Rather, it was just the culmination of hundreds of back and forth insults and jabs since the second grade.

They didn't like each other. Not at all. Stanley had hurled a vague insult in Ned's direction as they were leaving school, and the rest was history.

Ned glanced sideways at Stanley to see if he had an answer for Mr. Temple. Stanley's only answer was to put his left index finger against the left side of his nose and sneeze a long ribbon of blood onto the grass.

Gavin Temple sighed. "Graduation is in a week, boys. Do you really want to spend your final week at good ole MFH in detention?"

That elicited a quick, negative response from both combatants.

"I'll tell you what I'm going to do. I'm going to act like I didn't happen by here today. I'm going to give you both a chance to be better students for one more week. Then, you'll be off in the world, making both me and all of Middle Falls High proud to claim you as one of our own."

He looked from Ned to Stanley and back again, taking in their attitudes as he stared. His voice dropped an octave. "But if it doesn't work out that way, and if you make me regret that I'm giving you this chance, you will be the ones who end up being sorry. Are we clear?"

"Yes," Ned said.

Stanley nodded.

"Not good enough, Mr. Dill. I need to hear you say it."

"Yes, sir."

"Good enough. Shake hands like the young gentlemen I expect you to be from now on."

The two boys didn't make eye contact, but they did shake hands.

"Mr. Summers, you go along now. Mr. Dill, come back with me and we'll see if Nurse Billings can't find something to help with that nosebleed."

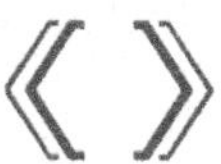

NED SUMMERS KNEW HE had caught a break. If he'd gotten in trouble for fighting, his father would have given him something even worse than anything Stanley could've thrown his way. A little bump on the head could be explained away, but a phone call home from Mr. Temple could not.

Ned hustled to the bike rack, pulled his old bicycle out, and pedaled home. He lived in a small, two-bedroom house less than half a mile from the school. It was in an area that had only been developed a few years before—part of the building boom in Middle Falls following World War II.

He rode down tree-lined streets. Eventually, those trees would grow up and form a canopy over Terrace Street, but today, they were just tall enough to provide a little shade on a hot, early summer day in Oregon.

Ned rode his old bicycle down the dirt driveway and leaned it against the back of his house. He ran in through the unlocked back door and into the kitchen.

Everything was quiet in the house, but that was almost always the case, even when he and his dad were both home. They didn't own a television yet. The radio had blown a tube a few weeks earlier and neither of them had gone to the store to get a new one. In addition to the lack of electronic noise, neither Ned nor his father, William, were especially chatty. It was possible, and common, for them to spend the whole evening together with only a few sentences exchanged.

Sentences like, "Pass the ketchup," and "Hey, shut that window, will you?" were much more likely to be said than a question like, "How was school today, Neddy?"

Those types of conversation had died with his mother, Nora, three years earlier. Not that she left them voluntarily. Five years ago, she was diagnosed with tuberculosis, which most people called *consumption* at the time.

She stayed in Middle Falls for as long as she could, but she ultimately went to a sanitarium in New Mexico in 1948. She died there before Ned could ever see her again.

The two men survived without her, although much of the light went out of their home. The garden and flower bed fell into disuse, dust piled up on every flat surface, and their weekly dinner menu became predictable.

Ned always got home before his father, so the cooking duties fell on him during the week.

He opened the potato drawer and pulled out a handful of the starchy vegetables. He peeled the potatoes, found a slice of thick bacon in the refrigerator, and put it all into the cast iron frying pan. His father had pulled a pound of hamburger out of the freezer that morning, so he formed the meat into thick patties and set them in the frying pan, too.

Just when Ned lifted the lid and peeked into the frying pan with the potatoes, the back door shut and William Summers walked into the kitchen. He placed a dented, black lunch pail on the kitchen counter. He walked over to the sink and ran some water into his thermos, setting it beside the sink to soak.

"Smells good."

Ned shrugged. "Smells pretty much like it does every night. I don't know how to make much else."

"Don't worry about that. It's kept us alive. I'm going to wash up."

By the time William reappeared at the kitchen table, Ned had dished up the potatoes and hamburger into equal portions. They sat on opposite sides of the table, with only salt and pepper shakers and a ketchup bottle between them.

In between bites, Ned cleared his throat and said, "Would you mind if I borrowed the truck tomorrow night?"

William looked up from his plate and took in his son. "Big plans?"

"I kind of have a date."

"That's not one of those things you kind of do. You've either got a date or you don't." William's words were plain, but there was no sting or rebuke in them.

"I've got a date."

William's eyes never left his son's, but he didn't say anything further.

"Mary Malone. I'm going to take her to the Pickwick to see *The Quiet Man.* It's got John Wayne in it, so I figure it's got to be pretty good," Ned continued to explain.

A faint smile touched the lips and eyes of William Summers. He reached into his back pocket and pulled out a worn billfold. He reached inside and pulled two singles out. He laid them on the table and pushed them to Ned.

"Oh, no, Dad. I don't need any money. I've got a few dollars saved from working at the store."

"That's good, but I've noticed you've been helping out with groceries with that money. Take her out for a milkshake after. There's that new place out on the edge of town. It's just a little shack, but the guys on the crew said they've got good burgers and shakes there. You save your money."

"Yeah. Artie's. I heard some kids talking about it, but I haven't been there yet. Okay, Dad. Thank you," Ned said, scooping the dollars up from the table. "I've got a little homework to do after the dishes."

William opened the front door, bent low, and picked up a copy of *The Middle Falls Chronicle*. "Don't worry about cleaning up. There's not many. I'll take care of 'em. You go ahead and get on your homework. Still giving you work just a week before graduation, huh? Good for them."

Ned didn't argue. He cleared the dishes off the table, placed them near the sink, retrieved his homework, and sat back down at the table.

Chapter Two

The next day, Ned did his best to avoid Stanley Dill. Their brief tussle had let off some of the steam they had built up, so he didn't think anything would happen. Still, he didn't want anything to mess up his date that night with Mary Malone.

Ned hadn't been on a lot of dates in his young life. In fact, unless you counted holding hands with Vera Adams at the roller skating rink the year before, he hadn't been on any at all.

When sixth period let out, he walked to the bike rack with his best friend, Stink Mitchell. Stink wasn't his real name, of course. It was Vernon. But he earned his nickname in the third grade. He'd had such an explosive bowel movement one day that the smell spread out in the hall. Considering his given name was Vernon, Stink wasn't that much of a downgrade.

Ned hadn't told Stink about his date with Mary yet because he'd been afraid to curse it, as if talking about it would somehow make it not happen.

Today, though, with the date in tantalizing sight, he took a chance.

"Want to hang out tonight?" Stink asked.

"Can't. Got a date," Ned said as casually as possible.

Stink faltered, gripped his chest dramatically, and nearly fell over. "Whew. That was close. For a second there, I thought you said that you, Ned Summers, the dateless wonder, would be going out with a girl tonight."

"Nah," Ned said, a smile lighting his eyes. "Not with a girl. A woman."

"Come on. Quit messing with me. What woman would go out with you?"

Ned drew himself up to his full five-foot-eight-inches and summoned whatever dignity he had. "I'm sure a lot of women would go out with me."

"Maybe, but only if you looked at the entire world's population. My question is how did you find one of them here in Middle Falls?"

Ned just shrugged and pulled his bike out. He swung his leg over and started to pedal toward home. He did so at a walking pace, though. He was enjoying torturing Stink, who had never gone on a date either.

"Come on," Stink said. "Play fair. Who is it?"

"Mary Malone."

Again, Stink stopped and feigned a heart attack. "Now I know you're ribbing me. Mary Malone? The girl from the grocery store? As in the Mary Malone who graduated two years ago? Drop-dead beautiful Mary Malone?"

Ned enjoyed his brief moment of triumph. Then he said, "No one is more surprised than me."

"Don't be so sure," Stink injected. "How did you pull it off?"

"I dunno. I guess I just...asked her."

"If only I'd known it was that easy," Stink said.

"Honestly," Ned said, leaning his head toward his friend, "sometimes I think it *is* that easy. I think maybe normal guys like us get intimidated by pretty girls and that's why we don't ask them out, which just leaves the jerks. After a few years of that cycle, maybe we start to look pretty good in comparison."

Stink looked at Ned through narrowed eyes, trying to determine if he was being straight or if he was actually pulling his leg. He gave up on figuring it out and just said, "You know what? Good for you. Good for us. Good for every boy that spent his whole high school life dreaming about girls like Mary Malone, but never had the guts to do anything about it." He slapped Ned on the back and turned right at the corner, heading toward his house. "Good luck, Romeo!" he shouted over his shoulder with a laugh.

"Thanks," Ned muttered to himself.

At home, Ned opened a can of corn and found that William had set some pork chops in the sink to thaw. He put them in the frying pan and turned the heat on medium-low.

No way I'm going to be able to eat anything, but Dad will be hungry when he gets home. It'll be a bonus night for him—he can have both pork chops.

Right at five-fifteen in the evening, Ned heard his dad's truck pull into the side yard, just like he did every night. A minute later, William walked in.

"Thought you might be too anxious for your big date to start dinner."

"No, just too anxious to actually eat it. You can have it all. I think I'm going to go wash the truck, and then take a bath."

William smiled at his son. "I put some gas in 'er this morning, so you're good." He pulled a plate out of the dish rack beside the sink. "They had something new at the gas station, too. They called it an air freshener. Looks like a little tree. I got one and put it in there, so now it doesn't smell so much like an old man's work truck."

Ned had a sudden urge to hug his dad, but he fought it. He couldn't remember ever hugging his dad. They had been building upon a tradition of not expressing anything for years now. Instead of hugging him, Ned nodded and said, "Thanks, Dad." On the back porch, he found a bucket and filled it up halfway. Placing the bucket under the kitchen sink, Ned filled it with some dish soap and water.

His dad's 1942 Dodge half-ton pickup was never going to be beautiful—he used it as part of his job, after all—but when Ned was done with it, it was clean at the very least.

He went back into the house and glanced at the clock on the wall above the stove—six-oh-five. He was supposed to pick Mary up at her house at seven o'clock, but right now, he was dirty and sweaty.

Thirty minutes later, Ned had bathed and changed into his best corduroys, along with a light blue dress shirt that had been hanging—untouched—in his closet for several years. When he put the shirt on, he was dismayed to find that it was tight across the chest. He had filled out over the years.

"Nothing else for it," he muttered as he looked for any other acceptable option in his closet. "This'll have to do."

He poured some Vitalis into his hand and rubbed it vigorously over his damp hair. Like every boy in Middle Falls, Ned had short hair. Rich and middle-class kids went to the barber, while the poor kids got clipped by their moms at home. Unless you were Ned. Then you got clipped by your dad.

Ned hadn't shaved, mostly because he didn't have much on his face yet. A few passes with soap and his dad's razor at the beginning of each week got him through just fine.

He poked his head out of the bathroom and shouted, "Hey, Dad! Can I use some of your Old Spice?"

"Sure you can," William said, and even though Ned didn't see his dad, Ned could tell he was smiling with amusement.

Ned splashed Old Spice into his hands. It mingled with the distinct smell of Vitalis, and Ned splashed it on his face and neck.

He tried to hurry through the living room, but as he did, William coughed slightly. The fumes roiled off him in waves.

"Do I look okay?"

"You're fine. Got your wallet?"

Ned patted his back pocket. "Yep."

"Have a good time," William said, then returned to reading *The Middle Falls Chronicle.*

Ned Summers was ready for his big date.

Chapter Three

Even though she worked full-time at the supermarket and had graduated high school two years earlier, Mary Malone still lived at home. Once a young woman graduated high school, she tended to stay at home and help out her family until she got married. Those who didn't snag a husband would live at home into their middle ages, at which point their parents died and the house became theirs.

There was little chance of Mary becoming an old maid, though. The only reason she was still single was that she had become adept at saying "no" to her suitors. She didn't know exactly what she wanted, but she knew it wasn't any of the opportunities presented to her so far.

Ned pulled up in front of her family's small, neat house at seven o'clock on the dot. Ned was always punctual.

In Middle Falls, Oregon, in 1952, if Ned had simply honked his horn and waited for his date to appear, Mr. Malone might have come out and wrapped the steering wheel around his neck.

Instead, Ned jumped down from the truck and made his way up the sidewalk to the Malone's front door. When he knocked, the door was answered almost instantly by a young girl, whom Ned recognized as being a freshman at Middle Falls. She had short hair and a wan complexion. It was possible she might grow into a beauty like Mary, but for the moment, she was stuck in an awkward phase.

"Mary, the victim of the day is here!" she shouted over her shoulder.

Ned searched his brain for the young girl's name but he came up blank.

Mary appeared around the corner, fastening an earring on her left ear. Ned's breath caught in his throat. He thought she was beautiful just standing behind the counter at the grocery store. Here, she was dressed in a soft pink sweater and a long gray skirt fastened with a black belt. Her dark hair curled softly around her face and her makeup was done, and as a result, she literally took Ned's breath away.

He smiled dumbly at her and tried to get his brain in gear and not embarrass himself. He did not succeed.

Unseen around another corner, a woman's voice said, "Well, bring him in so we can meet him."

Mary stood back, putting her hip into her little sister and moving her out of the way. She smiled a small apology at Ned, but she knew no man was going to get her out of her house until her mother got a good look at him.

Ned dutifully marched into the living room where Mrs. Malone was standing as she dried her hands on a dishcloth. Mr. Malone was hidden behind *The Chronicle* and didn't seem inclined to look at the newest boy to show up at his door.

Mrs. Malone reached a hand out to Ned, who shook it gently. "I'm Constance Malone."

"Nice to meet you," Ned said, reminding himself to make eye contact. He didn't want to be thought of as shifty.

"What are your parents' names? Might I know them?"

"Probably not. My mom died a few years ago— "

"Oh, I'm so sorry..."

"—and my dad works in construction. He's a heavy equipment operator."

That brought the newspaper down. "Local 701?" Mr. Malone asked.

"Yes, sir."

"Good organization. Good for him." The subject exhausted, Mary's dad returned the paper to its upright position.

"And what do you do?" Mrs. Malone asked. She was much more interested in Ned than Mr. Malone was.

"I'm just getting ready to graduate from Middle Falls High."

"Oh, I see," Mrs. Malone said, casting an unreadable glance at Mary.

"I've been working at Coppen's Hardware for the last year."

"That's very enterprising of you. Good for you. So many young people these days seem to lack the discipline to motivate themselves."

"They probably don't have a dad like mine," Ned said with a rueful smile.

The smallest of chuckles emerged from behind the paper.

"Well, fine. You two have a wonderful time. What are you doing?"

"We're going to a movie," Mary answered, long since ready to be gone from the house. It was unclear if she was trying to rescue herself or Ned.

"And then, if it's all right," Ned said to both mother and daughter, "I thought we might go by that new place, Artie's, for a milkshake. I think they're open until ten on Fridays."

"That would be dreamy," Mary said. "I love their milkshakes."

"Her last boyfriend took her there, too," her younger sister chimed in.

Mary aimed a short, swift kick in her direction, but her sister saw it coming and jumped back before running out of the room.

Mrs. Malone shook her head and said, "You know how children are."

As an only child, Ned didn't really know, but he nodded anyway.

Mary slipped her arm through Ned's and said, "Shall we go?"

"I'll leave the porch light on until you get home," Mrs. Malone said.

"I know, Mom," Mary said as Ned opened the door.

"Nice to meet you, Mrs. Malone. You, too, Mr. Malone," Ned said, but Mrs. Malone had already returned to the kitchen and Mr. Malone didn't so much as dip a corner of his paper in acknowledgment.

Out in the sweet late-spring air, both Mary and Ned took a deep breath.

"That's the worst part of the night, I promise," Mary said.

"It wasn't so bad," Ned said. He looked up and down the street Mary lived on. He was hoping against all odds that one of his friends would happen to ride by on their bicycle and see him walking arm-in-arm with Mary Malone. The street was unfortunately empty, though.

He opened the passenger side door for Mary and shut it behind her. He hurried around and slid in the driver's side.

When he looked at Mary, she had an odd expression on her face. "What is that interesting smell?"

Vitalis? Old Spice? Did I fart on the way here? Has it lingered?

Ned finally noticed the small green tree hanging from the rear view mirror and said, "Oh, my dad picked this up today. It's supposed to smell like a pine tree."

Mary thought for a moment and then nodded. "Yes, I see it."

Ned started the truck and used the shifter on the column to put it in gear. For the first time, Ned's stomach was really tied up in knots. He realized he was sitting in a car with not only a beautiful girl, but a beautiful girl who was also a complete stranger. Aside from a few thirty-second conversations at the market, they'd never spoken.

Mary looked out the window as they drove, giving no indication that she was going to start a conversation. Ned wracked his brain, looking for anything to say.

Nothing.

Chapter Four

The Pickwick Theater was a modern marvel, highlighted by an electric, neon sign in front that rose almost thirty feet into the air. There was a half-moon ticket booth in front where a middle-aged man in a crimson uniform and small hat stood, ready to dispense tickets. And get this. They were only twenty-five cents per person.

Ned didn't want to get what he normally did when he came to the Pickwick—a box of Milk Duds—because he was a little too nervous and he didn't want to pick at his teeth to loosen the caramel in front of Mary. Still, he nodded toward the concession stand and said, "Want something?"

"Yes, please," Mary said, as though she had been expecting the question. "I'd like a Baby Ruth and a small Coke, please and thank you."

They stood in line for a few minutes without talking. When they reached the front, Ned ordered and paid for Mary's candy bar and soda.

Okay. So far, so good. It's going okay. I need to be a little bit of a take-charge kind of guy.

"Let's go up to the balcony," he said, with all the confidence he could muster.

"Of course!" Mary agreed.

Ned breathed a small sigh.

They walked up the thickly carpeted steps to the balcony. The show was going to start in just a few minutes and the balcony was already halfway filled. Ned found two seats together on the left side of the front row and led Mary there.

While they waited for the movie to start, Mary unwrapped her Baby Ruth and slid it out of its wrapper. She took a tissue out of her purse and laid it across her lap. She then folded the wrapper and put it in her purse. She set the candy on the tissue and delicately began taking little nibbles from it.

Ned did his best to stare straight ahead but he couldn't help but glance at Mary out of the corner of his eye. Watching her slowly eat the candy bar was the sexiest thing he'd ever seen. Admittedly, he had led a sheltered life, but still, his heart was beating fast.

Mary sensed he was looking at her and she smiled innocently at him, not acknowledging the effect she was having on him.

A newsreel came on, showing Dwight Eisenhower on a whistle-stop train tour of the Midwest as a way of campaigning for his party's nomination for president. He was in a tight race with William Taft for the Republican nomination, but he looked calm and relaxed in the newsreel footage.

Definitely much calmer than Ned, who felt like the theater was closing in on him. The too-tight shirt, the incredible warmth of Mary's arm against his, and the image of her eating the candy bar made him sweat mightily, which caused the smell of Vitalis and Old Spice to surround anyone who was sitting within ten feet of them.

Ned was much relieved when a Looney Tunes cartoon came on because it gave him something to focus on. Immediately after the cartoon ended, the winged-eagle logo of Republic Pictures appeared on the screen and *The Quiet Man* began.

For the next two hours, Ned was able to partially forget about the warm, fragrant girl who sat beside him. Directly behind them was an amorous couple who made out throughout the entire running time of the movie, occasionally interrupting Ned's thoughts.

When the house lights came up, Ned looked at Mary and asked, "Well? What did you think?"

"So beautiful," she sighed. "Maureen O'Hara is the most beautiful woman in the world."

"Maybe after you," Ned said earnestly, immediately regretting it.

"Aren't you sweet?" Mary said, rewarding him with a smile that showed she was pleased.

As they exited into the cool night air, Ned said, "Still up for that milkshake?"

"You know it."

They drove happily out to the edge of town where a small building was lit up by the glow of the electric lights strung up around the parking lot. It was almost ten at night, but Artie's was still busy. They hadn't been the only ones to think of stopping by after the movie.

"Wait here and I'll get it. What do you want? Vanilla or chocolate?"

"I'll forgive that this one time, because I like you, but never ask me that again. Chocolate. Always chocolate."

Ned flushed as though he might have somehow stepped in it, but Mary let him off the hook with a small giggle.

"Right," Ned said, stepping down and closing the door.

Artie's wasn't much, at least not yet. Just a single big window for ordering, with a large piece of plywood propped up that shuttered it at night. A hand-printed sign hung below the window. It simply read *Artie's*.

Ned waited in line, enjoying the feel of the cool air. He glanced over his shoulder at Mary, who was primping her hair in a small compact. He had a hard time believing she was with him when she could have been with just about any guy in Middle Falls.

Music was coming from inside the little shack—*Cry,* by Johnnie Ray.

When he got to the front of the line, he recognized the boy behind the counter. It was Perry Zimmerman, a boy who had graduated the year before.

"Hey, Zimm, I didn't know you worked here."

"Hey, Ned. It's just for the summer. Going to college this fall, I hope, then I never want to see another hamburger again."

"I'll help you out, then. Two chocolate shakes."

"Two, huh? On a date? Good for you."

"Yep," Ned said casually. "Took Mary Malone to a movie."

Perry started scooping ice cream into a silver container, his eyes sweeping the parking lot as he did so. When he spotted Ned's pickup, he saw Mary. "Huh, how 'bout that? I thought you must be joking."

"That's pretty much everyone's reaction, yeah."

Perry finished the shake, poured it into two paper glasses, and stuck a straw in the middle of each. "Twenty cents."

Ned dropped a quarter on the plywood counter and said, "Keep the change, Zimm. See ya."

Ned and Mary sat in the parking lot, watching other cars as they came and went. Their windows started to steam up, so Ned cracked the wing window to let some fresh air in.

They finished their shakes in quiet. Ned made a mental note to plan out some things to talk about before his next date—that is, if he ever got another one.

Just as Perry Zimmerman was closing down and locking the plywood shutter, Ned started the truck and turned toward Mary's house.

Overall, it could have been worse. I could have spilled my milkshake down myself. I could have tripped and fell face-first into a curb. I could have said something stupid. Then again, it's not that tough to avoid saying something stupid if you never open your mouth.

They pulled up in front of Mary's house. It was all dark with the exception of the brightly glowing porch light.

"I'll walk you up," Ned said.

Mary shook her head. "You don't need to. My mom is watching us from the window right now."

Ned squinted at the window, but he could only see the curtains.

"I know she's pretty much invisible, but I promise you, she's there. Let's just say goodnight here." She looked into Ned's eyes, a mischievous glint making her even more fetching. "I can sneak out of my room and they won't even hear me," she confided. "I've done it before. Lots of times."

Ned couldn't help but wonder who the lucky guys were that she was sneaking out to see.

"But one date isn't enough to get me to sneak out and meet you," Mary said.

Since this wasn't something Ned would have even dreamed of suggesting, he wasn't let down by the loss.

"You'll have to earn that," she added.

Ned had no idea what to do, or what she meant by that. Out of sheer panic, he did nothing but sit as still as a statue. His father had told him again and again that it was better to be silent and thought a fool than to open your mouth and confirm it.

Mary leaned over to him and her faint perfume filled his nostrils, turning off whatever part of his brain that might have still been working. Her lips, warm and soft, pressed against his for a long, lingering moment.

Ned's eyes were closed, but every other sense was perfectly open and completely thrilled. A far-too-brief moment later, Mary and her perfect lips were gone and she was hurrying up the walk to her house. At the door, she turned and gave a little wave. Ned's heart gave a little lurch.

Some part of Ned's brain was functioning enough so he was able to put the truck back in gear after only two tries. He let the clutch out and slowly moved away from the Malone house.

He rolled the driver's window down and let the cold air rush over his hot face. He couldn't explain why, but all of a sudden, he let out a rebel yell into the quiet neighborhood. After doing so, he pulled his head back inside and, speaking to no one, said, "And that, ladies and gentlemen, was the greatest night of my life."

Ned spent the rest of the drive home planning how and when he could see Mary again.

NED WOULD NEVER SEE Mary again. At least not in this lifetime.

Chapter Five

Ned threw his leg over the seat of his bicycle and pedaled down the driveway to the street. From there, he turned toward downtown. His eyes had flown open before the sun was up and his fingers had unconsciously flown to his lips, feeling for a trace of the warmth Mary had left there the night before.

He headed to Coppen's Hardware for his normal Saturday shift. Mr. and Mrs. Coppen were among the hardest-working people Ned knew, which was saying something for Middle Falls in 1952. It was a place and a time filled with industrious people. The Coppens had owned the store since 1928. The booming economy of the Roaring Twenties departed shortly after they opened and the Great Depression arrived in its place. They persevered by doing every bit of work themselves, from open to close, six days a week.

World War II had brought more hardships, but Mr. Coppen was too old to go off to battle, so he had been around to help keep the doors open.

Owning a hardware store with a small lumber yard in the back was a good business in the aftermath of the World War II boom. By the late 40s, they had begun hiring high school kids to help out on the weekends. Ned was the latest of those kids, and he enjoyed the work, as hard as it was.

When he walked in through the back of the store, he took note of a small blackboard hanging on a nail. There was a list of jobs written in chalk—move plywood to rack, re-stack two-by-fours and six-bytwelves, and deliver six bags of concrete to the address of 1145 Denton. Ned ran his finger down the list and smiled. Mr. Coppen was no dummy. He arranged for lumber deliveries on Fridays, knowing Ned would be in to do the heavy lifting early the next morning.

Ned hollered, "I'm here, Mr. and Mrs. Coppen. Going to work now!" Then he walked out back to begin carrying and stacking half-inch plywood.

At three o'clock, Mr. Coppen came out back and surveyed Ned's work. His back was bent from many years of carrying nail boxes and heavy boards, but his eyes didn't miss a thing. If a stack of wood was off plumb at the bottom, it would be unstable as more was stacked on top. He took a full minute to examine everything, at which point he nodded and said, "That's good, Ned. See you next week."

Coming from Mr. Coppen, that was high praise.

Ned retrieved his bike and pedaled happily around town. Work was done, there was no school until Monday, and after next Friday, there would never be school for him ever again.

Ned had never considered going to college. He was an adequate student, but there was nothing that interested him about college.

The hardware store was never going to be anything more than a part-time job, so he knew he would have to find something else after graduation, but that was a problem for another day. On this afternoon, the sun was shining, he had a few coins in his pocket, and life was good.

He had tried to pretend like he was going for a leisurely bike ride around Middle Falls, but his pedaling inevitably took him toward the grocery store. He leaned his bike up against the front of the store as a bout of butterflies flew around in his stomach.

Ned held the door open for Mrs. Larkin and then he pushed into the store. Smith and Sons Grocery was the largest food store in Middle Falls, but somehow, it was still small and quaint.

The wooden floors were worn, the aisles were narrow, and the smell of produce, dairy, and meat hung heavily in the air. As soon as Ned's eyes adjusted to the dimness of the store, he glanced at the cash register. Ginny Smith, the old maid sister of the Smith clan, was there, ringing up a small line of customers.

Ned had long since memorized Mary's work schedule and knew that she usually worked on Saturday afternoons. That was why they had gone out on Friday instead.

Ned nonchalantly walked to the produce section and picked out several oranges. He wandered about the store for a few minutes, waiting to see if Mary had simply gone to the bathroom. After five minutes of circling the few aisles, he gave up and took the oranges up to Miss Smith.

In the most off-handed way he could muster, Ned said, "Thought I might see Mary here. She usually works on Saturday, doesn't she?"

The pinch-faced Miss Smith didn't even look at him. "Irresponsible kids today. Boys always coming in looking for her. She didn't come into work today and she didn't even bother to call or send her sister to let us know."

Ned nodded, picked up the small paper bag with his oranges, and walked away. The warm sun had moved behind a cloud and it felt like the temperature had dropped several degrees since the last time he stepped outside.

Is she sick? She felt fine last night. We both drank a milkshake at Artie's, but I feel fine. Maybe she had some bad food at home before we left. Maybe I should go to her house and check.

As Ned biked toward the Malone house, he saw so many kids outside playing, jumping rope, enjoying hopscotch, and tossing jacks. He slowed as he approached the Malone house. It felt wrong to arrive at Mary's house on a bicycle after he had driven the pickup the night before. It was like a demotion of sorts. Ned pedaled past the house, did a slow U-turn, and rode by again. Everything seemed quiet and undisturbed at the Malone house. Their car was in the driveway, and the curtains were open, but there was no one visible inside.

Ned shrugged and headed for home. *I could call her when I get home instead. Or, I could try to not be a goof and just wait until tomorrow when she's scheduled to work at the grocery again.*

Ned never shied away from hard work, but postponing social niceties that he did not understand came much easier.

He arrived home just in time to start dinner. He had it ready when his dad returned home after running his Saturday errands. Ned braced for the inevitable onslaught of questions, but William only said, "Smells good," as he did almost every night.

They ate in comfortable silence, although his father did glance at him from time to time as if he thought Ned might volunteer something about his big date the night before. In the waiting game, they both emerged as winners.

Ned cleared the dishes and then retrieved his homework. "Almost done with this," he said, pointing to his English book, "then I probably won't have any more homework ever again."

William nodded. "Have you given any thought to what comes next? We've got an apprentice program, if you're interested. It won't make you rich, but it will keep you fed and provide for a roof over your head. You can stay here as long as you want, but eventually you'll want to strike out on your own."

"Thanks, Dad. That wouldn't be so bad. I like to do things with my hands. I'll give it some thought."

"Whatever you want to do is fine, as long as you do something."

Ned finished writing the last paper of his high school career, said goodnight to his dad, and turned in for the evening. He closed his bedroom door behind him and turned out the light, but he laid in the darkness for more than an hour before sleep found him.

POLICE CHIEF MICHAEL Deakins rolled his prowler into his driveway. Police Chief was a good title, but in Middle Falls, it just meant a lot of long hours for not a lot of pay. Deakins and his two deputies were the only full-time cops in town.

He turned the engine off and sat quietly for a few moments, gathering himself. It was just past midnight and the streets were deserted. He hoped that his wife, Sandy, was already asleep. After the events of the previous night, he didn't want to talk to anyone—especially her.

He slipped his key into the lock of the front door and let himself into the small entryway of their single-story home. He loosened his gun belt, rolled it up tight, and put it at the top of the coat closet. He stepped into the living room, and from there, he could see the light of a lamp in the bedroom.

He poked his head inside. "Still awake, huh?"

"Couldn't sleep. What kept you out so late?

"Mr. and Mrs. Malone reported their daughter missing this afternoon. I spent the night driving around and looking in all the normal places. I was hoping to find her and send her home, but I didn't find anything."

"A missing girl in Middle Falls has to be a runaway, right?" She called Mary a girl, even though Sandy was only a handful of years older. Mary was still living the life of a girl, whereas Sandy was married, settled down, and part of the adult fabric of the community.

"Likely," Michael said, nodding.

"I saw her last night. Pretty late, too."

"What? You did?"

"It's hard for me to go to sleep when you're not home. I spend a lot of time in the rocking chair, just looking out as I wait for you."

"What was she doing? Was she alone?"

"No. She and a boy were driving by, but for some reason, they pulled over and sat there for quite a while. It looked like they might have been having an argument."

"Did you recognize the boy she was with?"

"No, it was too dark. I only recognized her because the streetlight was right above her."

"I don't like the sound of that. I'll have to do some more investigating tomorrow. Until then," he said, standing and stretching, "I'm ready for bed."

Chapter Six

The next morning was Sunday, but William and Ned Summers hadn't attended church ever since Nora left for the sanitarium. Instead, Ned got dressed in old clothes, fired up their old lawnmower, and ran it over what passed for their front lawn. It was patchy and showed the long inattention that had been paid it, but in the springtime, the grassy parts grew fast.

He was nearly done when a Middle Falls police car pulled up to the curb in front of their house.

Ned recognized Michael Deakins. Most everyone in town knew the youngest-elected Police Chief in Middle Falls' history. He had been a decorated war hero who came home to continue battling the forces of evil—or, at the very least, keep the juvenile delinquents and town drunks in check here on the home front.

"Ned Summers?" Deakins asked.

"Yes, sir."

"I need to ask you a few questions."

Ned stepped around the lawnmower and opened the front gate for Chief Deakins. "Sure, of course. Let's go inside the house," Ned said, wiping the sweat off his forehead with the back of his arm.

He led Deakins up the steps, through the front door, and into the modest living room. It was arranged just as it had been the day Nora Summers left for New Mexico four years earlier, albeit covered in a thick coat of dust.

Ned didn't sit or offer Deakins a chair. Instead, he just looked at him, waiting.

"I need to ask you a few questions about Mary Malone. Her parents said that you and Mary went on a date on Friday night. Is that correct?"

"Yes," Ned said, a growing feeling of anxiety in the pit of his stomach. He tried to think of any reason a cop would be at his door and asking about Mary, but none of the answers he came up with were good.

"Where did you go on your date?"

"We went to the Pickwick, and then for a milkshake over at Artie's."

Deakins nodded. "I'll admit that I've stopped there for a late night snack more often than I should since they opened up. My wife's been telling me those shakes and burgers are going to make me fat." He patted a non-existent bulge above his belt. "Then you took her home, right?"

"Yes, sir. I dropped her off a little after ten."

"Mrs. Malone confirmed that, yes."

So, she was *watching us through the curtains after all. Mary was right.*

Deakins pulled a small notebook out of his back pocket and referred to it. "Mrs. Malone said she knew that Mary sometimes came home from a date, but would then sneak back out to see the boy she had been with."

Guess you weren't as quiet as you thought you were all those times after all, Mary.

Ned knew there was no question there—just a statement—so he continued to look Deakins directly in the eye. The police officer smiled. It was a slightly conspiratorial smile that implied something along the lines of, "We're all boys here. We can level with each other." He cleared his throat. "Did Mary sneak out to meet back up with you?"

"No, sir. I let her out at her house and then I came straight home."

"Did your mother or father see you come home?"

"My mother is dead and my father was already asleep when I got home."

Deakins slipped the notebook into his back pocket and took a step toward the front door. He laid one hand on the doorknob before he turned and said, "Anything unusual happen on your date?"

Mary Malone kissed me, and that was pretty unusual, but I don't think that's what you mean.

"No, nothing unusual. I stopped by the grocery store to see if she was there yesterday afternoon, but Miss Smith said she wasn't at work.

"No, she wasn't at work yesterday. No arguments or anything?"

"No, not at all. We had a nice time."

"One last question... What did you pick Mary up in?"

"My Dad's Dodge pickup truck. Can I ask why you're here? Is Mary okay?"

Deakins made a note in the little notebook. "I'm sure she is, but she's missing at the moment. I think it's likely a miscommunication between her and her parents. But they've reported her as missing, so I am talking to everyone who saw her on Friday to see if I can piece together what's going on. If you think of anything significant about your date on Friday, call down to the office, okay?"

"Of course."

Ned watched Deakins climb back into his car and pull away.

Mary Malone, what is going on with you?

She didn't leave Ned's thoughts for the rest of the day, but aside from stewing about it, there wasn't much he could do. At school the next day, what should have been the beginning of a final victory lap before graduation took on an ominous tone for Ned. He half-expected Mary's disappearance to be the talk of the school, but if anyone mentioned it, it wasn't in his presence.

By sixth period, Ned had decided that he would ride around town before he headed home. Maybe he'd stop by the grocery store and ride past Mary's house again. Fifteen minutes before the dismissal bell rang, there was a knock on the classroom door. The principal, Mr. Bolton, stuck his head into the room and scanned the class. His eyes settled on Ned.

"Mr. Summers, can I see you for a moment?"

Ned stood up and took a step toward the door. As he did so, Bolton added, "Why don't you grab your books, too?"

A murmur ran through the class, which only intensified when Bolton stepped aside to show Chief Deakins standing behind him.

"Who'd ya murder, Summers?" Stanley Dill stage-whispered behind him.

Ned ignored him and gathered up his belongings. Of course, by trying to hurry, he dropped the top book off his stack, which landed flat on the floor with a resounding boom. That caused another round of twitters and laughs. Ned flushed, grabbed his book, and hurried through the door.

"Yes, sir?"

"Chief Deakins wants to have a few words with you. I've told him he can use my office."

The three of them—tall, athletic, gun-carrying, uniform-wearing Deakins; balding, short-sleeves-wearing, tie-adorned Bolton; and young, stocky, Ned in his white T-shirt and jeans—made an unusual trio walking down the hall. At the principal's office, Bolton opened the door and let Deakins and Ned inside, closing the door behind them.

Deakins didn't sit behind Bolton's desk, but instead, he indicated a straight-backed chair next to Ned and took a seat in a similar chair next to him. He watched Ned with eagle eyes, taking in every hair that might be out of place and looking for even the most subtle shift in Ned's demeanor.

The two sat and stared at each other in silence while the clock above Bolton's desk ticked away the seconds. *If he's expecting me to blurt something out, we're gonna be here for a long time.*

Finally, Deakins said, "Ned, Mary Malone has been found."

Relief flooded through Ned's body. "Oh, that's great. I was starting get really worried when she hadn't shown up yesterday and—"

Deakins held his hand up to stop Ned. "No, that's not what I mean. Mary's body has been found. She's dead."

Chapter Seven

Ned sat completely still. A wave of surprise started at the top of his head and ran down his spine. It brought a sudden onset of nausea.

He had been worried about Mary. He had considered that she might have run off to Portland or Seattle to start a more exciting life. She always seemed a little bigger than the small town she had been born into. He thought that she might have snuck out to meet one of the boys she had dated previously and just decided not to come back. He even wondered if maybe she'd borrowed a car and run off into a ditch somewhere but was unable to get out to find help.

He had never, ever considered that she might be dead. Aside from his mother, Ned didn't know anyone else who had died. And Mary? Mary was young, healthy, and vibrant. Confident and full of life. Which meant that she didn't just keel over. Something happened to her.

"How? What happened?"

Ned realized that Deakins had not taken his eyes off him for the previous minute, while he was working through everything.

"I can't say."

"But..." Ned trailed away. Ned did his best to pull himself together. He took his questions, boxed them up, and put them into a deep recess of his brain where he could take them all out and consider them later. He finally came up with just one question.

"Why are you telling *me*? We only had one date. I don't think I'm all that high on the priority list."

"Aside from her mother seeing her through the living room window, you are the last person to see her alive. You were the last person to spend any time with her that night. I have some questions for you."

That gave Ned a jolt. "Wait. Do you think I did it? That I killed Mary?" His voice climbed an octave, betraying how incredulous he found the idea.

Deakins sat stock still, his eyes still probing. He didn't confirm or deny that question, which was a type of confirmation in and of itself, and Ned knew it.

Ned looked up at the ceiling. "Damn. Damn."

"You didn't ask me where she was found."

"If I did, would you tell me?"

"No."

"Then why do you want me to ask?"

"It just seems like a normal question someone would ask."

"Nothing feels normal. Someone killed Mary Malone. There's nothing *normal* about that."

"You're assuming that someone killed her. I didn't say that."

What? Are you saying that Mary killed herself? No way. Absolutely no way. She was too happy and too full of life for that.

"I can't believe Mary would kill herself, so I assumed someone did it. I understand that I was the last person to see Mary. But I had nothing to do with this. I liked Mary a lot. We had a really nice night. She kissed me goodnight before she went in the house. There's no reason I would hurt her." Ned still hadn't wrapped his head around the fact that she died, and saying *there's no reason I would kill her* felt surreal.

"It's still early on in our investigation. We're not assuming anything yet. I'll be in touch with you."

Ned felt dismissed, so he stood up. "I'll do anything I can to help you find out who did this."

"Thank you, Ned. Right now, the best way you can help me is to make sure I can find you when I need you."

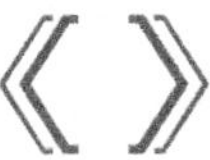

THE NEXT FEW DAYS DRAGGED by for Ned.

A week ago, he'd wished that everyone in school could know that he had a date with the beautiful Mary Malone. Now that everyone knew, he wished they didn't.

When he walked down the hall, people looked at him strangely. People he had gone to school with since kindergarten crossed to the other side of the hall when he approached, or they'd whisper to their friends as he walked by.

Even when he went to the store to get something for dinner, he saw people taking notice of him. He had gone from total Middle Falls anonymity to a kind of celebrity he didn't want and a fame he couldn't appreciate.

On Friday, Ned rode to graduation with his father. Neither of them owned a proper suit, but they both wore their best clothes—right down to their matching bolo ties.

As they drove to school, William said, "I've been worried about you this week."

"I know, Dad. I understand. I just don't know how to handle this. I don't know what to do."

"I don't think there's anything *to* do except wait. I'd like to say everything will turn out just fine, but that can't happen, can it? That young girl is dead." William pulled into the crowded Middle Falls High parking lot and turned the engine off. "You got plans for after?"

"No. There's a big party somewhere outside of town, but I don't feel like going. I'm just gonna head home with you, if that's okay."

"Sure it is, but I thought maybe we could stop somewhere and grab a quick bite to celebrate. Oh, and I almost forgot to give you this," William said, opening the glove box. "I'm proud of you, son." He pulled out a rectangular white box and handed it to Ned.

Ned slipped the top of the box off and found a pocket knife with a rough-pebbled handle. He opened the knife and turned it left and right, catching the light on the steel blade.

"That's so great, Dad. Thank you."

"I know it's not much—" William began, but Ned broke down and grabbed his father around the neck, silencing the protest. He held his father for a long moment, resting his head in the crook of his neck.

Chapter Eight

In 1952, Middle Falls, Oregon had a population of 26,457 people. It was, in other words, a quintessential small town.

Like small towns everywhere, there was much to recommend it and many perks of living there. Neighbors looked out for each other. People tended not to parade their troubles out in public, but instead, they did their best to keep their issues invisible behind tasteful curtains.

Mary Malone's murder was something different altogether. It was the number one topic of conversation in every café, hair salon, and barber shop, as well as the subject that most dinners revolved around. Within a few days, virtually everyone in town knew the details of the murder.

Mary had been found in a copse of pine trees that circled the newly-constructed Whitaker Park. There was a service road that ran alongside those trees, so the working theory was that Mary and her unknown killer had driven there. The thought was that they stopped there and found somewhere to park beneath the deep shade of the trees.

Mary had been shot with a small caliber gun—a .22, to be specific. A wound from a gun of this nature wouldn't have necessarily been fatal, but the bullet buried itself in her heart. Doctor Haskins, who performed the autopsy, said she had died almost instantly.

All those things were facts, and yet everyone in town endlessly dissected them. From there, the conversation veered off into suppositions and theories. The theoretical explanations focused intently on Ned Summers. Quite a handful of other boys had dated Mary, but the spotlight didn't settle on them the way it did on Ned. Most of the others had moved on with their lives. They all had girlfriends or fiancées of their own. Those who were still single had strong alibis to account for where they were on that fateful Friday night.

None of those things were true of Ned, and more and more often, the attention of the town turned to him. He might have eventually escaped the glare of the spotlight if Constance Malone hadn't run into Sandy Deakins at the post office. Of course, Mrs. Deakins offered her sincere condolences to Mrs. Malone over the loss of her daughter.

Mrs. Malone had grown used to accepting the sympathetic looks and expressions of sadness, but as time went on, she found them more of a burden than a comfort. Still, she bore up under her grief and thanked each person for their thoughtfulness.

After Sandy shared in the grief for a moment, she said, "I'm sure Michael has told you what I saw that night."

Like a starving prisoner jumping for a crust of bread, Constance said, "No, he didn't. What did you see?"

Sandy looked at the sudden longing on Constance's face and her mouth twitched. "Oh, I shouldn't have said anything. I'm just not used to Michael dealing with anything like this."

"What did you see?" Constance repeated. Now that the information had been mentioned, she wasn't going to budge until she heard it. All of it.

"It's probably nothing," Sandy said, backpedaling. "Just that I saw Mary that night, a little after midnight. She was riding with someone who happened to pull off the street and park for a few minutes right in front of our house. I was waiting for Michael to come home like I always do, but that night, I saw your daughter briefly."

Constance took a step toward Sandy and laid a hand on her collarbone. "Did you see who she was with?"

"No," Sandy said, shaking her head. "It was dark. A streetlamp just happened to illuminate Mary's face, so I knew it was her. I couldn't see the driver at all."

Constance's face fell, but just like that, it brightened again. "What were they riding in? What kind of car?"

"It wasn't a car at all. It was an older pickup. Not one of the new and shiny ones, but an older model. I can't identify the model. I'm such an idiot about things like that."

"And you told Michael about this?"

"Of course. We don't keep anything from each other."

"Of course." It appeared that Constance was reeling. She hadn't learned anything in the two weeks since Mary's murder. It was obvious she needed to think about this new development. She hugged Sandy quickly and said, "Thank you," then retreated out of the doors of the post office.

That conversation was on a Friday morning. Within twenty-four hours, almost everyone in Middle Falls knew that Mary had been seen in an older pickup. It didn't take any longer than that for people to start talking about Ned Summers and speculate about his father's work pickup.

Sandy's indiscretion caught up to her at home as well.

"Sandy, did you tell Mrs. Malone about what you saw?" Michael Deakins had no more than stepped through the door of their modest home as he asked the question. He was once again taking his gun belt off and putting it in the closet.

Sandy had been sitting in her armchair, reading her copy of Redbook, but she put it down on the side table and stood up. She bowed her head. When she looked up at Michael, there was obvious pain in her eyes.

"As soon as I said something, I knew I goofed. But there was no denying Mrs. Malone. As soon as I let it slip that I saw Mary that night, she wasn't going to take no for an answer. I would have given anything to take those words back, but it was too late."

Michael shook his head. "This is an unusual case. You're not going to be a possible witness in a crime like this very often. But I need you to be more discrete. What we talk about here in the house, regarding the death of Mary Malone, can't ever leave the house." He reached down and lifted her chin, pulling her face up to him. "Understood? It's part of being married to the chief of police of Middle Falls."

Sandy nodded emphatically. She changed the subject, saying, "I made a roast for dinner."

THE COLLECTED WISDOM of the town was that Chief Deakins would make an arrest soon, and that it was Ned Summers who would be sent to jail. But that wasn't the end of the talk. Everyone believed Ned would be tried for murder, and after being found guilty, he would end up in prison—maybe even on death row.

Ned Summers, who had lived a completely anonymous life for eighteen years, had become infamous in Middle Falls. But time moved on and Ned was not arrested. In fact, no one was. That did not stop the jury of the good people of Middle Falls from coming to a verdict.

In the court of public opinion, Ned was found guilty.

Chapter Nine

It was three o'clock in the afternoon on the last Saturday in June of 1952. Mr. Coppen was having a hard time making eye contact with Ned.

Coppen cleared his throat which did not need clearing and searched for the right words. He didn't find them, but he spoke anyway. "We're going to have to call this your last day, Ned." He handed Ned his pay envelope, which contained his pay for the last two Saturdays, plus a little extra.

Perhaps Ned should have seen this coming. High school boys working for Coppen's Hardware rarely worked there beyond the summer after they graduated. Mr. Coppen liked to hire and train the new boys that would get him through another school year.

In this case, that wasn't why Mr. Coppen was letting Ned go.

Ned understood, but he couldn't help himself. He asked, "Why?"

Mr. Coppen's eyes flitted away to the rotating rack of different-sized nails. He was nervously looking around at various items, including the boxes of hinges and the sprinklers hanging in the lawn and garden section. Resolutely, he finally looked Ned in the eye. "It's nothing you've done. I don't believe for one minute what people in town are saying. But I'm losing business. People are telling me they'd rather drive half an hour away than come to a store that..." his voice trailed off. He had lost his momentum.

"That has a murderer working in it?" Ned ventured.

"Yes. Exactly. I'm sorry, Ned. I just can't afford to lose any more business. If I do, I'll have to close the doors."

"That's okay, Mr. Coppen," Ned said, even though it wasn't okay. It wasn't okay at all. Working at the hardware store had been something he always looked forward to, especially now that everything else was a chaotic mess. At home, he tended to follow his own thoughts round and round, falling down a dizzying hole with no resolution. If he went anywhere in town, people pointed, crossed the street to get away from him, or simply stared at him. He thought the hardware store would always be his escape, but now it wouldn't be. Now, it felt like he had nowhere he could go.

"I've been planning to apply for an apprentice position with my dad's union, anyway. It's probably time for that." Ned squared his shoulders and offered the best smile he could force. "Thank you to you and Mrs. Coppin for letting me work here. It's been the best."

Ned retrieved his bike from the lumber yard and pedaled toward his home. It was a warm and sunny day, but more than ever, it felt like the walls were closing in on Ned. He took a detour on his way home and rode past Whitaker Park, which was exactly where Mary's body had been discovered.

He knew he should probably stay away from there. If people saw him walking around the area, they would assume he was only there for ghoulish purposes. Still, he was drawn to the area time and time again. On a conscious level, he knew that the area had been processed like a crime scene. Chief Deakins and his deputies had already gone over the area one blade of grass at a time, looking for clues and information.

On a completely subconscious level, he didn't accept that. Part of him believed that if he just looked a little more closely, he would find the piece of evidence that everyone else had missed. After tromping around in the long grass, looking up into the trees, and searching for God only knows what, Ned gave up and rode back home.

Half a block away, he noticed Chief Deakins' squad car parked at the curb. When he pedaled closer, he saw that Deakins and his father were standing in the front yard, talking. Ned coasted into the driveway, dropped his bike, and walked toward them.

His father spoke first. "Chief Deakins wants to ask you some questions, but he wants you to go down to the station with him. What do you think? You don't have to go—the Chief made that plain. But it might help settle some of these ridiculous questions."

"I don't mind. I didn't do anything." Ned looked up at Deakins, who was half a head taller than either he or his father. "But I don't know what good it will do. I've told you everything I know."

Deakins nodded sympathetically. "I understand. It would be helpful if you came down voluntarily, though. We might be able to clear the air about a few things."

"Okay, let's go," Ned said. "Can you give me a ride home afterward?"

"Of course. Mr. Summers, I'll bring him back after he's answered our questions."

Ned stood by the back door of the car, but Deakins said, "Come on, you can ride up front with me." Deakins climbed in, leaned across the seat, and threw open the front passenger door.

He picked up his radio mic, said, "En route," and then clicked off before they drove to the station.

DEAKINS PARKED IN THE space marked "Chief" at the Middle Falls Police Station. It was a small, boxy building just a block off the main drag. Deakins led Ned inside, walked him through the glass double doors, and shuffled past the receptionist, who tried—but failed—to not stare at Ned.

"Right this way," Deakins said, pointing down a narrow hallway. "We're going to go in that second door on the right. It ain't much, but it's what we've got."

That room wasn't exactly a coat closet, but it wasn't your typical interrogation room, either. It was seven feet by seven feet, which was just enough room to fit a heavy metal table and two chairs. One of those chairs was filled by the slight figure of a short, balding man.

"Ned, this is Bob Asher. He's with the Oregon Criminal Bureau of Investigation. We don't get a lot of murders in Middle Falls, so Bob has come from Salem to help us out. He's got a lot more experience than we do."

"Hello," Ned said.

Asher was reading a file and didn't look up when Ned and Michael entered. He pointed to the empty chair across from him, saying, "Take a seat."

"I'm gonna let you two talk," Deakins said, excusing himself.

Got a bad, bad feeling about this. Seems like Deakins can't get it done, so now they've brought in the big guys from the state, and their attention is focused on me. But that's fine. I've got nothing to hide.

Chapter Ten

When Asher finally looked up from the file, Ned noticed watery blue eyes behind thick glasses. He wore a white shirt as well as a tie that was loose at the collar. Asher gave every indication that he'd been studying the case intently for several hours.

"I've read your statement, but I'd like to go over a few things with you," Asher said.

"Sure, no problem. Whatever I can do to help."

Asher *said*, "I'd like to go over a few things with you again," but what he *meant* was that he wanted to go over every single thing Ned had ever told Deakins. It took almost an hour to go over Ned's previous statements word-by-word. When he got through with that, Asher flipped the pages over and started the whole routine again. Any time he found a minute difference in what Ned had said, he zeroed in, going over it again and again.

I'm glad I don't have anything to hide, Ned thought. *If I did, I'm pretty sure this guy would find it.*

There was a clock on the wall opposite Ned and he realized he had been in the tiny, almost airless room for two hours. At that exact moment, Asher said, "I need a break," with a tinge of disgust in his voice. Just like that, he walked out of the room.

Ned turned his face toward the door as it opened, happy to breathe in some air that hadn't been recycled a dozen times. He sat alone for fifteen minutes until Deakins came back in. "Hey, I just noticed we've got you here after dinner. Deputy Cline is going to run out and get us all hamburgers. I feel bad keeping you here so long. Can we get you one?"

Ned was hungry, but he felt like if he ate something, he might be letting himself in for an even longer stay. He shook his head. "Thanks, Chief, but I'd rather eat with my dad when I get home."

"Suit yourself," Deakins said. "How about a Coke then? We've got a machine down the hall."

Again, Ned shook his head.

Deakins left Ned alone in the small room with nothing to do but watch the second hand of the clock go around and around.

As if on a schedule, Asher came back in exactly fifteen minutes later.

He was still intense, but it was obvious he was doing his best to soften his demeanor. He attempted a smile, though it didn't fit well on his homely face.

"Look, Ned. We've got a lot of information now." He paused, as if taking the measure of the young boy in front of him. He leaned forward. "We already know what happened. We just need you to confirm it for us."

"If you know what happened, that's great, but I can't confirm it for you, because I don't know what happened."

Asher went on as if Ned hadn't spoken. "We know how these things go, and I am sympathetic. Sometimes, these situations just get out of control and things that you never planned end up happening anyway. You'll help yourself out in the long run if you just tell us everything."

Ned held firm. "I've told you everything you need to know."

Ned had the right to an attorney, but he didn't know it. Asher sure didn't tell him, either. If Ned had ever watched television, he might've known, but he hadn't. In 1952, less than ten percent of the homes in America had a television. When it came to Middle Falls, that number was much lower. The only television Ned had ever seen was in the window of Coleman's Furniture store. He had been to movies at the Pickwick, but that was mostly to see western serials. In short, he had no idea how interrogations worked and he was definitely not aware of the good cop, bad cop routine.

Asher leaned in closer. Eventually, he was so close that the smell of stale coffee on his breath was unavoidable. "Like I said, son, we already know what happened. We just need you to tell us in your own words."

Ned stared back at him without answering, so Asher opened the file yet again. "Okay, let's start at the beginning again, then."

This routine—asking Ned to relay his story again and again, giving him a chance to confess, and switching places with Deakins—went on for three more hours.

Ned hadn't eaten anything since his bowl of oatmeal before going to the hardware store. He also hadn't slept well the night before, but that wasn't unusual. He hadn't really had a good night's sleep ever since finding out that Mary had been killed. He wanted nothing more than to lay his head down on the hard surface of the table and drift off to dreamland.

"Do you have any guns in your house?"

This was a new line of questioning, which perked Ned up a little bit. "Of course," Ned replied.

"What do you have?"

"There's quite a few. My dad and I hunt. We've got a .410 shotgun for pheasants and grouse. We have a .30/06 for deer hunting. We've also got a couple of .22s for target practice and shooting at rats as well as squirrels."

"You guys have a .22, eh? Rifle or pistol?"

"Both."

"Has Chief Deakins looked at either of them?"

The light dawned on Ned. "Oh, right. Someone killed Mary using a .22-caliber gun, didn't they?" Ned drew a deep breath, trying to focus. "No, as far as I know, Chief Deakins hasn't looked at either of ours."

"Would you mind if he did?"

"I wouldn't mind, but I can't give permission for that. They're my dad's guns. You'd have to ask him."

Ned looked up at the clock. It was nearly midnight.

"It's late. Can you tell me when are we going to be done here? I want to get home," Ned expressed.

"We can be done right now if you just tell me what happened that night."

Ned felt a swell of emotion rising up inside of him. He'd told them everything he knew, over and over and over, but they didn't believe him. They were never going to let him out. He was going to be in this small, sweaty room forever.

Maybe I should just make something up so this can be done.

The door opened and Ned could see that Asher was taken by surprise. Whatever schedule they had set up, this wasn't part of it.

Deakins stuck his head in and said, "We're going to have to let Ned go now."

Irritation gave way to anger on Asher's flushed face. "Why? We're not done yet."

William Summers burst into the room. "If you want to keep my boy here one minute longer, you're gonna have to arrest us both. If you're not prepared to do that, we're going to walk out of here." He stuck his chin out defiantly, looking from one man to the other, daring them to say something.

Ned had rarely seen his father angry, but heat radiated off him as he challenged the two bigger men.

Deakins took one step back and William took that as an answer. He gestured to Ned to come to him, and Ned gratefully did. After sitting for so long, Ned's first few steps were stilted and unsteady. William offered his arm to him for support.

The elder Summers pierced Deakins with a look. "Next time you come around all friendly-like and want to talk to my boy, you're gonna get a different reaction. I'm hiring a lawyer on Monday morning. You can direct any questions to him."

He put his arm around his son and led him out into the cool night air.

They climbed into the Dodge. William started it and pulled out onto the deserted street.

"I never should have let them take you away without me. Deakins made it sound like they would have you home by supper."

"I didn't think they were ever going to let me go."

"Next time they come around the house, they'll see the business end of our thirty-aught-six, or so help me, God."

"I don't think they're ever going to leave me alone, Dad. They've got their aim set on me, and for some reason, no one else will do."

They rode in silence the rest of the way home. The Dodge's headlights lit up the driveway and then their small house.

"I don't think I can take this anymore, Dad. I've gotta get out of here."

Chapter Eleven

Ned and his dad didn't talk any more that night about what Ned meant. It had been a long, exhausting day, and all Ned wanted was the comfort of his own bed. There was a time earlier in the evening when he thought he might never have a chance to see his bed ever again.

The next morning, he felt the pall of the previous night's interrogation weighing on him like a psychic hangover.

When he wandered out of his bedroom, he realized how completely unmoored he felt. He'd had the strict schedules of school, sports, and work at Coppen's Hardware to help him plan and structure his week. Now, looking at the week ahead, he had nowhere he needed to be. The highlight of each day would be his father coming home after work at five-fifteen.

The smell of bacon sizzling on the stove drew him to the kitchen.

"You've got to be starving. Did you eat anything after breakfast yesterday?" Ned's dad asked him.

"No. They offered to get me a hamburger at the police station yesterday, but it didn't feel right taking it," Ned rationalized.

"Good boy. I'd have done the same thing," William said.

William pulled three pieces of bacon out of the pan with a fork. He added three spoonfuls of scrambled eggs as well as some toast with butter. He handed the heaping plate to Ned. "Here's to a better day today."

"Thanks, Dad." Ned took two steps toward the dining room, then stopped and turned around. "I just don't know if it will be, though. I still don't have a job. People stare at me like I'm a murderer no matter where I go. A few weeks ago, you said something about being able to get me into the apprenticeship program at the union. Is that still on?"

William averted his eyes for a moment. He dished up his own breakfast in silence. Then, he said, "Sit down. Let's talk about it."

When they were both settled into their chairs, William said, "I guess I don't have as much pull as I thought I did. They rejected your application a few days ago. I just hadn't wanted to tell you."

Ned didn't react for a moment. Instead, he just blankly stared off into space. Eventually, he spoke up, saying, "That's it then, isn't it? Other than you, there's really no reason to be here."

"Last night, you said something about getting out of here. What do you mean? Out of where? Middle Falls? Oregon? The West Coast? Where?"

"No, nothing quite that drastic," Ned said, crunching on some bacon. "I'm thinking of the hunting cabin."

That stopped William in mid-forkful. "The cabin? It's pretty rough."

"It is, but it's still summertime. It'll be warm, and it won't rain as much," Ned explained. "I won't have anything but time on my hands. I can start fixing it up. You've taught me a lot about how to do things. No matter what, we'd end up with a better hunting cabin when I'm done with it."

The cabin was William's inheritance from his father. He had been staying there during deer and fishing season ever since World War I erupted. It had been almost that long since he had made any improvements there. There was no running water and certainly no electricity, not to mention the roof leaked a little more every winter.

They promised themselves they would fix it up each summer before hunting season, but then other things inevitably became priorities and it was pushed back another year, and then another, and another. It was barely sufficient for two men to camp out for a few days each fall, let alone for one young man to live in on his own.

William was quiet for a few minutes while he finished his breakfast.

Ned was an adult, but he didn't want to make such a major decision without his father's stamp of approval.

Finally, William stood up from the table and took his plate into the kitchen. He wiped his hands on a dish towel and then he turned, giving Ned a look that held equal parts understanding and sadness.

"I've got a bunch of materials that I've been saving up to work on the cabin one of these days. Looks like that day is today. Let's go load the truck."

An hour later, they had the Dodge half-ton loaded with lumber, tar paper, tools, and bags full of nails.

The cabin was at the end of Forest Service Road about twenty-five miles outside of Middle Falls. If you followed FSR-227 until you reached the dead-end, you would see an ill-kept spur road just one hundred yards before the turnaround. Down that spur road was the Summers' hunting cabin, but you could only reach the destination with a vehicle capable of getting you there.

Almost an hour after they left their house, they pulled up in front of the cabin and William had to laugh. "It looks even worse in the sunshine than it does in the rain."

"Looks pretty good to me," Ned said. He scrambled out of the pickup, grabbed his sleeping bag, and put his shoulder into the front door. There was no lock. Not even a latch.

"If you stay out here for a long while, we're gonna have to get you a lock," William said. He reached up and touched the splinters that shot out of the top of the door. "Hell, maybe even a real door for you."

Inside was a single room, twenty feet by twenty feet. Just to the left of the door was what passed for the kitchen. It was comprised of an ancient wood stove and a piece of lumber between two saw horses, which functioned as the countertops. Old apple and peach boxes were nailed to the wall, serving as cupboards. There were two old beds with sway-back mattresses but no blankets. There was no bathroom.

"We're gonna need to dig you a latrine," William mentioned.

"Plenty of time to do that, and plenty of free labor," Ned said, pointing to his right bicep.

"Good thing," William said, looking around at the decrepit interior. "Well, come on, Mr. Free Labor. That roof ain't gonna patch itself."

Chapter Twelve

William spent the rest of that day working alongside Ned. Once they got started, the awkwardness of the situation faded and they were once again just father and son, working side-by-side, as they had done for so many years.

When darkness settled in, William wiped his forehead with his red handkerchief and looked back on what they had accomplished. There were fresh patches of tar paper over the known leaks and they had done the best they could to shore up the foundation in the areas where it leaned the most.

"Everything else will have to wait for another day. I was hoping we would get a lot more done today." William said. He looked at Ned, who was sitting on the top step and leaning back against the door frame. He looked content.

"You coming home tonight?"

"I think I am home, Dad. It feels like it. For right now, at least."

"I thought you might feel that way. There's a box of groceries in the back of the truck. That'll last you a few days. I won't be able to make it out every night, but I'll be out a few times this week, so I'll bring you more supplies then." He reached in the cab of the truck and pulled out the zippered case that held the .30/06 Springfield. "You need to hold on to this. I don't want you staying out here without it."

Ned took the handle of the case and said, "Sure, Dad." He leaned it inside the front door, then cocked his head and said, "I'll be fine. You brought more than enough food to get me through, and the river's close enough, I can hear it gurgling. This is good. I'll be living the life of Thoreau."

"That reminds me. I'll bring along my book that identifies plants and berries in western Oregon next time I come. In the meantime, if you don't recognize it—"

"Don't eat it," Ned said, finishing the advice for him. "I know, Dad. This isn't my first time staying in the woods."

"No, it's not, and I'm glad, but it is your first time staying out here alone."

"Nobody's going to bother me all the way out here. This will give me a chance to clear my head and think about what I want to do next."

William held his son's gaze for a long moment and opened his mouth to say something else, but he swallowed his words. Instead, he simply lifted his hand, climbed back in the truck, and drove away.

Ned watched until the taillights of the pickup had faded completely. Ned went inside and did his best to close the door behind him, but it didn't quite fit in the jamb.

"Job 1-A tomorrow," Ned said. His voice sounded odd in the quiet of the cabin. There were no windows, so there wasn't even any light coming in from the moon or the stars. He fumbled around, looking for the matches on the makeshift countertop so he could light the kerosene lamp, but he couldn't find them. Finally, he gave up and decided to just turn in and start fresh in the morning.

WILLIAM DIDN'T MAKE it back to the cabin until Thursday night. When he rolled up, Ned was using a hand plane to shave a little off of a board.

"Whaddya think?" Ned asked, waving his hand expansively.

"I think it looks a lot like it did when I left on Sunday night."

"Ouch. My blisters and sore back disagree. There's a latrine with a makeshift toilet out back, the door actually closes now, and I'm reinforcing the rafters that are threatening to give way."

William lifted a cardboard box out of the back of the truck. "Brought you some food. Figure you're about out by now."

"If I'm gonna stay here long, I'm gonna have to get my trap lines going. Rabbit stew sounds pretty good."

"How about pan-fried trout?" William asked, hauling a spinner pole over the tailgate and lifting up a creel and a tackle box.

"It sounds a lot better than another peanut butter sandwich, that's for sure. Come on, let's walk down to the river and see if anything's biting."

They walked the winding path away from the cabin. William noticed half a dozen trees that Ned had felled and stacked up beside the house.

Ned followed his gaze and said, "Gonna get cold this winter. I'll need wood. Better to think about it now than in October."

"That's my son."

An hour later, they walked back up the path with a steelhead and a couple of smiles.

"I could get used to this," William said.

"Retire, sell the house, and move out here. That would be pretty great." Ned's tone was joking, but his facial expression hinted that he might be serious.

"No," William said. "My life isn't here. It's in town. I can't leave my job. But I will never leave my son, either. I will come out every chance I get until you decide to come back home."

They filleted the steelhead, built a fire in the old fire pit out front, and set the frying pan on a steel grate. They didn't have a lot of spices, but salt and pepper on a steelhead that had been swimming an hour earlier made for a great meal. They ate as much as they could and still had too much fish left over.

"You don't want to leave that around. What you don't eat will attract the kind of attention that you don't want."

"I think my next job is to build a smoker. I'm never going to have refrigeration out here, but if I got a smoker up and running, I could keep enough meat to get me through the winter."

"I've got plans for building a smoker at home. I'll take a look and bring some more lumber next time I come out."

"You driving home tonight?"

"No. I took tomorrow off, so I can stay here and help you get things a little more ship-shape."

They had no interest in working more tonight, though. They sat in two folding chairs around the crackling fire and waited for the stars to come out. They had full bellies and longed for nothing else but this moment.

Chapter Thirteen

When Ned had decided to move out to the cabin, it was a spur-of-the-moment decision that carried no long-term plan along with it. He only wanted to escape the whispers and stares that greeted him wherever he went in Middle Falls.

As the days rolled by slowly, Ned had a hard time finding a reason to return to paved streets and houses. He had never been the social type as he naturally restricted himself to just a few friends at a time. Until he'd gone out with Mary, he'd never even thought of having a girlfriend, so not having one again was no shock to his system.

When he first moved out to the cabin, he didn't have so much as a radio, so he made his own entertainment. He was surrounded by forest on all sides, which meant he had all the wood he would ever need to build most anything he wanted. If he needed a planed board for something specific, William brought it to him during one of his visits.

After Ned had been in the woods for a month, they both realized that he wasn't planning on returning to town—at least not in the immediate future. With that in mind, they made plans to make the cabin as winter-proof as they could.

First, they built a wood smoker so that Ned would be able to keep meat and fish edible without refrigeration. Then, they patched holes in the walls and made a weather-resistant insulation out of mud and moss. They made more permanent repairs to the roof so that it wouldn't leak during the rainy season, which was always long in Western Oregon. Finally, they built a small log structure around the latrine Ned had dug so he wouldn't be doing his business in the wind and rain.

When the weather started to turn in September, Ned brought a number of saplings inside and used the days to make himself furniture—a table, chairs, and a new bed. After that, he taught himself to whittle. At first, he made simple things, like a whistle, or a pipe for his dad. Eventually, he moved on to carving the animals he saw every day. Finally, he carved a checkerboard and pieces so he and William could play chess during the long winter evenings.

Aside from his dad, Ned rarely saw other human beings. From time to time, a truck would drive all the way to the end of Forest Service Road, but they typically just turned around and retreated to town. On rare occasions, someone would drive down the spur road until they reached his cabin.

In mid-September, Chief Deakins drove all the way in and parked in what Ned thought of as his front yard. Ned was outside, skinning a rabbit he had caught, and heard the car coming for quite some time before it appeared.

Deakins got out of the prowler and leaned against the roof of his car, watching Ned work.

"Something I can do for you?"

"I heard you were out here. Just wanted to come have a look for myself."

"Got more questions for me? Want to go over my statement a few dozen more times?"

"I'm sorry about that, Ned. We're under a lot of pressure to solve this. That's why we brought someone in from the state."

Ned stripped the fur and dropped it beside him. "Well, now you know I'm here. You could have just asked my dad."

"I did. I stopped in at his place a few weeks ago. He told me to get the hell off his porch." Ned smiled at the image, and eventually, so did Deakins. "I had that coming, I suppose."

"I suppose so."

A long silence settled on the two men. Deakins looked up at the tall firs that surrounded the cabin. The wind made them sway and give off a gentle whoosh. The sound of the river burbled.

"I kind of envy you being out here."

"It wasn't my choice. I had other plans. But now, I'm happy here. If you need me, you know where to find me." Ned picked up the remains of the rabbit, went inside, and closed the door behind him. A minute later, he heard the prowler fire up and retreat to town.

In October, William took a week off to go deer hunting, just like he did every year. They got a buck the first day of the season and spent the rest of the week skinning and butchering it. They carried the intestines and unusable bits far away from the cabin, constantly aware of bringing unwanted attention from bears, coyotes, and big cats. They ate well the rest of the week and smoked enough to last Ned through most of the winter.

William brought him supplies he couldn't make himself, like flour, coffee, sugar, and potatoes. On the night before William returned to Middle Falls, they sat around the table in companionable silence. The only sound was the warming fire crackling and popping in the old wood stove, along with the occasional hoot from an owl outside.

"As soon as we get a few dry days, I'm going to clear an area out back so I can start planting a garden. I don't want to have to count on you to always bring me my vegetables. Between fishing, hunting, and trapping, I can keep myself in meat, but I need those vegetables, too."

"I thought when the winter was over, things might have quieted down in town, and maybe you could come home."

Ned stared into the flickering flame of the kerosene lantern. "Maybe. I don't know if it's ever going to quiet down. Our town has a long memory."

The two of them hadn't spoken about Mary's murder in months. There was no reason to.

"Anything new at all about the murder?" Ned asked.

"No, nothing. People are still talking about it, but they tend to shut up when they see me."

"That's what I mean. I don't know if they'll ever forget. What would I do with myself if I was in town? I don't think anyone's going to want to give me a job. I can't just hang around the house polishing the silver all day."

They both smiled at the idea, since neither of them had polished the silver since Nora Summers had passed away.

"In the woods, I've got things to keep me busy all day. There's always more projects to work on than I have time for, and I like it that way. If I came back to town in the spring, do you think the union would accept me as an apprentice?"

"I'd like to think they would, but I'm not so sure anymore."

"That means if I want to get a job, I've got to move to another town. Like Springfield, or Eugene, maybe. And that means I'll get to see you a lot less than I do now." Ned stood up and fetched the battered old coffee pot off the stove, filling both their cups. "I think I'll ride it out here for a while."

Chapter Fourteen

As it inevitably does, time passed. That first year spent fixing up the cabin turned into another and another.

The world away from the cabin changed. The Korean War ended during the summer of 1953. Before the United States had recovered from that conflict, Eisenhower was already approving a built-up military while simultaneously warning against becoming involved in another Asian country, called Vietnam. Less than a year later, the U.S. began sending military advisors to assist the South Vietnamese government.

Ned's world changed very little. He became a little leaner on his diet of meat and vegetables. But the forest and the river remained unchanged. He took some comfort in that. A crow or an owl might scold him when he intruded on them, but they never spoke about him behind his back.

William bought Ned a tiny transistor radio for Christmas in 1955. It was a modern marvel. "I bought it for you so you can listen to the newscasts from KMFR, if you want to kind of keep up with what's going on in the world."

Ned knew that it was an expensive gift and thanked his dad profusely. Even so, when his father returned home, the radio mostly sat on a shelf. Ned wasn't concerned with the news of the world, and he much preferred the symphony of sounds that surrounded him in the forest.

The one constant in Ned's life was his father. He never went more than a week without William stopping by for at least a few hours, and they spent most weekends together, either trapping, fishing or just sitting around a fire.

Those visits stopped abruptly in October 1959. Ned had been in the cabin for seven years by then and he truly thought of it as home.

William made his normal trek out to the cabin the first weekend of the month, but then two weeks passed and he didn't come back.

Ned knew something was wrong, but he felt helpless to do anything about it. After the second weekend passed with no sign of William, Ned knew he had to return to town. He wished that he had thought to have his father drop off his old bicycle, but he hadn't. Too late now.

It was twenty-five miles back to town. Ned knew he could walk at a steady three miles per hour over the even ground of Forest Service Road, so it would take him a little more than eight hours of steady walking. He was still young, and he was in great shape from working and hiking around the cabin, so he knew he could do it.

He waited through Sunday afternoon, hoping he would see his dad's old pickup come up the road with a laugh and a good story about why he had been away.

When darkness fell that night, he was still alone. Ned didn't sleep much that night. His stomach was in knots and the best he could manage was to doze off for a few minutes now and then. Finally, while the moon was still high in the sky, he put the few things he was going to bring with him into a small canvas backpack and left.

When he was only fifty yards away, he turned and looked back. The little cabin stood in the deep shadows of the night. Ned drew a lungful of the cold October air and turned on his heel.

When he was living at the cabin, he never wore his watch, because time was meaningless to him. There were no programs to catch and no appointments that he might miss. He ate when he was hungry and slept when he was tired.

This day, though, he listened to the little transistor radio his father had bought him, waiting for them to announce the time. Then, he set the watch and slipped it around his wrist.

He left the cabin at four-seventeen in the morning.

His eyes adjusted to the dark, so he never felt the need to turn on the flashlight he had brought with him.

The horizon in the east was just starting to lighten when he stopped to sit on a fallen log and drink some of his water. He only sat there for a moment before he was back on his feet. He had a terrible feeling that his father needed him.

By noon, his stomach was growling, so he sat on a large rock on the side of the road and ate some of the jerky he had made from the deer that he and his dad had shot earlier that month. By the early afternoon, he made it to the end of the Forest Service Road and onto the two-lane highway. After being away from people and civilization so long, the number of cars passing him by was unnerving. He was also afraid that people driving by would recognize him, but no one did. He had let his hair grow out and his beard had come in, so it was unlikely anyone would connect this lean, bearded drifter with the young man Middle Falls had once known.

The first thing he noticed when he got to the edge of Middle Falls was that the Artie's hamburger stand was gone. The little white shack was leveled and there was a much larger building in its place. A tall sign towered above the building and flashed "Artie's" in bright, neon yellow, with "Burgers and Shakes" in red beneath that. There was a large parking lot around it, and as he watched, a pretty, young woman with red hair emerged from inside and brought food to one of the cars.

Ned had never seen such a thing, but he didn't even consider stopping in and placing an order. Instead, he continued on toward his house. After traveling so far, the remaining distance seemed like nothing. He walked right through the heart of Middle Falls and not a single person seemed to recognize him.

He turned off the main drag through town and walked straight toward his childhood home. When he saw it in the distance, his heart beat a little faster. It looked completely unchanged. Even his dad's old Dodge half-ton sat in the driveway. He broke into a run and drove his tired legs onto the porch. The door was locked and the inside of the house was completely dark.

Ned pounded on the door and hollered, "Dad! Dad! it's me! Are you in there? You okay?"

He peered in the window to the living room, but there was nothing to see. The house inside looked completely unchanged.

This doesn't make any sense. Why would your truck be here without you?

Ned ran around to the back of the house and found that the back door was unlocked. This was typical, though, for they had almost never locked that door.

He burst into the kitchen, shouting "Dad!" There was no answer. A strong feeling of dread gripped him and slowed his feet. He had a sudden vision of his father lying dead on his bed.

With trepidation gripping his heart, he walked to his father's bedroom door and pushed it open. The bed was unmade, and the covers and sheets were thrown back haphazardly, but nothing else was out of the ordinary.

Ned's heart settled into a normal rhythm and he took a slower tour of the house. Everything seemed to be in place, aside from a table lamp that had been knocked over. Ned reached down and picked up the lamp, then sat down on the old couch, trying to think of what to do now.

He unlocked the front door and stood on the front porch, looking up and down the street.

"Ned? Is that really you?" It was a voice from off to his left. An old man's voice.

"Yes, it's me." Then he said, "Wait. Mr. Randolph? Is that you?"

"I almost didn't recognize you! You've been gone so long. And you look so different!"

Ned's hand flew up to his shaggy hair. "Do you know where my dad is?"

"Of course. He's in the same place he's been for weeks now. He's at Middle Falls Hospital. Last I heard, he was in Intensive Care."

"What? What happened? Do you know?"

Randolph shrugged through the gathering gloom. "Don't rightly know what happened to him. An ambulance came and hauled him away. I thought you'd moved away. I didn't know how to call you."

He was speaking to Ned's back now, as Ned had run back into the house and slammed the door behind him. He found the keys to the Dodge hanging right where they always did and he sprinted toward the truck.

Chapter Fifteen

Ned ran into Middle Falls Hospital and headed straight for the information desk, which was occupied by a woman in a starched white uniform.

"I need to see if my dad is here," Ned gasped. He had a hard time catching his breath, partly from running, mostly because he had a fear he was too late. "William Summers."

"One moment. Let me see." She turned a page in the large record book placed in front of her. Then she turned another page. And then another. "Yes, he's a patient here. According to this record, he's been here for several weeks."

"I just found out. What room is he in?"

"He's in 1427, but visiting hours are over for today. You'll need to come back in the morning. Visiting hours start at ten."

Before she finished her sentence, Ned was running down the corridor, looking for Room 1427. He took two wrong turns and momentarily ended up in the maternity ward, but he eventually found the correct room.

Standing outside, Ned was almost afraid to open the door and see what waited on the other side. He glanced at the end of the hall to see a nurse and an orderly marching straight for him, which gave him the courage he needed to step inside the room.

Inside, he saw his father lying in the hospital bed. He looked much thinner than the last time he had seen him and he needed a shave. The bed had been made around him, but he was so still that Ned couldn't tell if he was deep in sleep or if he was dead.

Ned stumbled to the bedside and watched his father's chest, waiting for it to rise. It finally did.

The nurse and orderly stepped inside and hoarsely whispered, "You're going to have to leave now."

Ned's arrival hadn't woken William, but the whispering caused his eyes to fly wide open. There was momentary fear in his eyes, as if he wasn't sure which world he was waking up in—this one or the next. When his eyes focused, they rested on Ned. He tried to wrestle his arm out from under the sheet and reach for his son.

The orderly took several quiet steps toward Ned, but William's hoarse voice said, "Stop. Stop. This is my son. I've been so worried about him."

"Mr. Summers, it's too late at night and we can't have the other patients bothered."

William waved his hand weakly around the room. There was another bed beside him, but it was empty. "What patients?" He gathered his strength and tried to sit up. "If you won't let Ned stay here, I'm going to get up out of this bed and go home with him right now."

That sounded like a wonderful idea to Ned, but the nurse said, "Don't be ridiculous, Mr. Summers. Fine." She turned her attention to Ned. "You can have five minutes with him tonight, but then you'll have to come back in the morning. Come, Jerome."

William collapsed back in the bed and Ned could see what that little bit of activity had cost him.

"Dad, what happened?"

William didn't answer immediately, but instead, he reached his hand out. Ned grasped it and held on, but it felt different to him. Wrong. As if his dad's strength and vitality were gone.

"They say I had a heart attack. I don't know. A few weeks back, I was in the house and it felt like someone had slipped a vice over my chest. I couldn't breathe, so I called the hospital and they sent an ambulance to get me."

"I should have been there with you."

"Let's not play that whole angle. It could have happened when I was miles out in the woods and up on the side of a hill. What would you have done with me then? Dragged my old carcass back to town?"

"You know I would have."

William tried to muster a laugh, but it just wouldn't come. "I suppose you would have at that." A thought flitted across his face. "Speaking of, how did you get to town?"

"How else? I walked."

"Today?"

"Yes. I started this morning before the sun came up. I went to the house looking for you, but Mr. Randolph told me you were here."

William nodded, but his eyes grew heavy. "Why don't you head on home now? Come back in the morning and we can talk more."

"I don't want to leave you alone."

"I'm fine, boy. Go on home. Get a meal and a night's sleep. Your room is just like you left it. Come in the morning and we'll plan the next time I can come out. I want to see what else you've done since I've been gone."

Ned pulled his father's hand up and rested it against his cheek. His eyes bore into his father. "It's funny. We talk so much every time you come out, but right now, it feels like there's so much I want to tell you."

"Good enough. Tomorrow. Plenty of time tomorrow." William closed his eyes.

Ned stood still for several minutes, holding his father's hand and watching his chest slowly rise and fall. Finally, he gently laid his dad's hand down. He didn't tuck it under the sheet. That had looked too much like a corpse to Ned's eyes.

Ned didn't want to leave, but he knew there was nothing else he could do. They obviously wouldn't let him curl up and sleep in the empty bed next to his father.

He took one step and realized that his muscles, as young and strong as they were, had almost reached their limit for the day. He walked stiff-legged to the truck and made his way home.

As he drove through the town, he noticed small things that had changed in Middle Falls. Old buildings had been torn down and replaced with larger ones. Areas that had once been filled with saplings and blackberry bushes now had row after row of seemingly identical houses.

By the time he got to what had once been his home, he was too tired to even open a can of pork and beans. Instead, he got a glass of water from the sink and carried his little pack into his old bedroom.

Ned had been gone for seven years, so the small, neat room felt foreign, not familiar. The bookshelf that held his baseball glove and small knick-knacks from school felt like they were from another life altogether.

He sat on his bed and took another piece of jerky from his pack. Before he could even take a bite, he was asleep.

Chapter Sixteen

Ned woke up having to pee badly, and then he quickly realized he was also thirsty, hungry, and sore. He took care of everything but the muscle soreness, knowing that it would ease with time.

He didn't want to make a scene like he had the night before, so he made himself wait until ten in the morning before he arrived at the hospital for visiting hours. In the meantime, he made a breakfast of eggs and Spam, and then he drove around town. He was pleased that no one seemed to recognize him.

I'm sure that would change if I was here again permanently.

He pulled into the Middle Falls Hospital parking lot at ten on the dot. This time, he didn't need to stop at the desk, and he didn't take a side trip to the maternity ward, but instead, he walked straight to Room 1427. When he poked his head in, he saw an old man in the bed next to the window, but his father's bed was stripped and it had crisp white sheets stacked on top.

"Oh, sorry," Ned said to the old man. Ned took a step back. He double-checked the room number. It was the correct room. An intense pain started high in his chest and settled in his stomach. He ran to the nurse's station.

"Excuse me. I think my father's been transferred to another room. Can you tell me where I can find him? William Summers. He was in Room 1427 just last night."

The pretty, young nurse smiled at Ned and said, "Let me see what I can find." She grabbed a clipboard with room assignments, flipped a page, and ran her finger down it. Her smile froze in place. "Have you spoke to his doctor?"

"No, I got here late last night. I was hoping to talk to him this morning."

The nurse nodded, a sympathetic expression on her face, which hurt Ned far worse than any slap would have. "I'll see if I can find his doctor."

"Wait, just... Wait. Please tell me. Is my dad all right?"

The nurse was caught on the horns of a dilemma. She didn't say anything, but she allowed herself a small shake of her head, eyes downcast.

Ned backed away from her until his back was against the hallway wall.

I just saw him last night. He put his hand to his forehead to stop the world from spinning. *That's right. I saw him last night, and how did he look? He looked like death.*

Ned hadn't cried since he had found out his mother had died, but the tears came now, running hot and fast down his face. He couldn't face the nurse. He didn't want to be in the hospital any longer. He didn't want to be anywhere except home. The vision of his cabin nestled sweetly in the woods called to him.

He hurried to the front doors. To his truck. To the edge of town. He was almost to Forest Service Road when he caught himself.

I can't do this. I owe it to him to take care of things.

He pulled onto the shoulder, did a three-point turn and headed back to the hospital.

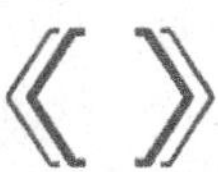

NED SPENT SEVERAL WEEKS in town, taking care of things. The last thing he wanted to do was plan a funeral, but he knew his father was well loved at his job and that he had old friends who deserved the chance to pay their respects.

At the funeral, an older man approached Ned and introduced himself as Trip Hartley. His card actually read, "Court Hartley III, esq." Ned guessed that was where the "Trip" came from.

He shook Ned's hand, gave him his card, and said, "I'm so sorry about the passing of your father. He called me when he was in the hospital and wanted to make sure I had everything taken care of for you when this time came. Can you come visit me in my office tomorrow? Say, around three? The address is on the card."

Ned had wondered how he was ever going to handle all the details that needed to be attended to, so he quickly agreed.

There was a much bigger crowd at William Summers' funeral than Ned had expected. His union brethren showed up in full force, as did many others from around Middle Falls—his barber, the men from down at the garage, and the small group of men he had coffee with on Saturday mornings. An attractive older woman who Ned had never seen before came up to him after the service and told him what a wonderful man William was. He had no idea how she knew his father.

Ned saw Chief Deakins, a little older and with the slightest of paunches developing over his former athletic frame, but he ignored him.

Guess my protector is gone, Deakins, so you can come get me, if you want to. But Deakins just stood in the back of the church, watching the proceedings. He left without saying a word.

The next afternoon, Ned was in Hartley's law office a few minutes before three, as instructed. An attractive, middle-aged woman showed him into an office where Hartley sat, a folder on the desk in front of him.

The wall behind him was lined with bookcases, each filled with heavy law books.

"Ned," Hartley said, getting straight to things without preamble, "I didn't know your dad well. He had already had his heart attack and was in the hospital when he called me. I visited him there several times. He gave me a key to your house and told me where to retrieve some of the papers I have here."

Ned nodded. "I'm sorry, but why am I here? Is there something I need to sign?"

"Did you know your father had a life insurance policy?"

"No, no idea. He paid all the bills."

"It's not a huge policy, but it's for $25,000. He took it out right after your mother died, so you would be taken care of if he passed suddenly."

Ned's eyes filled with tears. Not at the thought of the money. That meant virtually nothing to him. It was just another way that his father had taken care to show Ned just how loved he was.

"Then, there's the house. Your father made the last payment on the mortgage a few years ago, and he willed it to you. Once the inheritance tax is paid, you'll own it, free and clear. Aside from the property taxes, you can live there forever at no charge."

"I don't want to live there."

Hartley opened the file in front of him, flipped through a few pages, and said, "Your father said you might feel that way. Apparently, you live in a little place out in the woods?"

"Yes."

Hartley's eyes took on a faraway look. "Wake up to the sound of the river every day, and go to sleep serenaded by the hoot owls? I envy you." He jerked himself out of his reverie. "In any case, your father willed both the house in town and the cabin in the woods to you, free and clear. If you don't want the house, you can sell it. Or, you can appoint me to handle the sale for you, and I will. For a reasonable fee, of course."

"I went through the house the last few days. I took everything I want out of it. It all fit in the cab of Dad's old truck." Ned reached in his pocket and retrieved the keys. He laid them on Hartley's desk. "I never need to go back in there. You can sell it with everything in it."

Hartley retrieved the keys. "Very good." He slid a saving's book across the desk. "I took the liberty of opening an account for you. I'll deposit everything directly into it. It's hard to predict the real estate market, but when all is said and done in a few months, I'd guess there will be close to forty thousand dollars in it.

Ned nodded, but other than that, he didn't really react. "Is that everything? I'd like to get home. I've been away for too long and I want to check on things before it's completely dark."

HE PULLED HIS DAD'S Dodge—which he had to remind himself was now *his* Dodge—to a stop in front of the cabin, just before dark.

The little shanty still leaned a little, but the roof was good, the door shut properly, and most importantly, Ned knew he was home.

Chapter Seventeen

Ned Summers was never again questioned in the murder of Mary Malone, at least in that lifetime. Over time, it became a cold case. It was never forgotten about, but the investigation was no longer active.

It was a shocking crime, but even the most spectacular stories burn out when there's no oxygen to keep them alive. The facts that Ned moved out of town, and that no new clues or tips surfaced, allowed the case to recede into the history of Middle Falls. Eventually, Mary became nothing more than a cautionary tale that parents told their children. *Don't stay out too late,* they'd say. *Remember what happened to poor Mary Malone.*

Ned lived in his cabin in the woods for the rest of his life.

He was alone until the spring of 1962, when a mangy black lab wandered into the cabin from off of Forest Service Road. Ned had no idea who she belonged to, but she was skinny, except for her heavy stomach, which swung ponderously from side to side. She padded up to Ned and softly licked his extended hand.

"Somebody dump you off, girl? Guess they didn't want to feed you and however many puppies you've got in there."

Ned looked at her appraisingly. There was a hint of some other breed in her, but he had no idea what it was. He didn't have any dog food, of course, but he fed her a can of green beans, which she wolfed down and looked for more.

"Let's slow down on the chow, old girl. We'll have some more in a little while."

A few days later, the dog—who he had named Chark, because she was the color of burned charcoal—climbed onto the second bed and gave birth. She had carried four puppies, but one was stillborn. The remaining three were as dark as their mother.

Ned hated going to town—his skin felt itchy from the time his truck tires hit pavement—but he drove in and stocked up on powdered milk that he could feed Chark, along with every kind of dog food the store carried.

The pups grew up to be healthy and strong, and Ned went from being a loner to being the leader of a small pack almost overnight.

He took Chark into the vet and had her fixed. Eventually, he did the same with the three boys—who he named Huey, Dewey, and Louie—as soon as they were old enough.

Chark died in 1969, but her three offspring each lived for another five years. Once one of them died, the second followed close behind. Louie couldn't stand being the only four-legged pack member left, so at one point, he simply laid down and refused to eat. Ned buried them side-by-side in a shady spot behind the house.

He could have gone to the new pet store in Middle Falls and gotten another dog, but he never did. Chark had found him and trusted him with her pups, and in a way, it had felt like karma. With them gone, Ned returned to his solitary life.

He was alone, though he never really felt lonely. He missed his dad most days, and he thought of his dogs often, too, but Ned never felt the need to seek out any other companionship.

The turbulent decades of the sixties and seventies passed by, leaving barely any mark on Ned. His dad's old Dodge pickup, which he used for his monthly supply run to town, finally gave up the ghost in 1970. He replaced it with a newer model—a 1960 Dodge pickup. Thankfully, Ned spent little and he never had to worry about money.

Ned was occasionally spotted by hikers and other interlopers. He had stopped shaving and cutting his hair many years before, so he wondered if he might be at the root of some of the Sasquatch rumors he heard about when he listened to Art Bell on his AM radio late at night.

Eventually, someone made a sign and hung it where his road veered off from Forest Service Road. They had hand-painted "Hairy Man Road" and drawn an arrow pointing toward his cabin. "Proceed with caution" was also painted on the signage.

The change in the world began to speed up a little bit in the eighties and nineties. Computers became more commonplace, followed by the Internet.

Ned's concession to encroaching technology was to buy a gas-powered generator in 1982 and string an electrical line for a single bare bulb that hung from the ceiling. After being without electricity for thirty years, it felt like quite a luxury to be able to switch a light on whenever he wanted.

In December of 1999, while the rest of the world was worried about Y2K, Ned marked his sixty-sixth birthday. Ned heard stories of the upcoming apocalypse on the radio, but he wasn't worried. If all the technology in the world stopped working, he would barely notice.

There were times he looked back at his life and wondered how it would have been if he hadn't worked up the nerve to ask Mary Malone to go see *The Quiet Man*. He usually came to the conclusion that life would have been different, but he wasn't sure it would have been better.

On June 17, 2004, Ned woke up feeling poorly. He decided to take it easy that day and put off his chores until the next day. However, he felt worse the next day, and the next, too. On the fourth day, he woke up and realized he couldn't move the left side of his body. When he looked in the mirror, he saw that the entire left side of his face was frozen. Both his left eye and that side of his mouth had drooped.

He wasn't in such poor shape that he couldn't have managed to drive himself into the hospital in town, but he had long ago decided against that. Instead, he slowly made his way out to a spot by the river where he knew western water hemlock grew. He picked a basket of it and took it back to his cabin. Even though it was a warm summer day, he lit a fire and put the kettle on to boil.

When it whistled, Ned poured the steaming water over the hemlock and let it steep. He pushed the leaves and tubers down with a wooden spoon, forcing their brownish poison out into the water. He waited for it to cool, then used the spoon to lift the leaves out and onto the table. He took one experimental sip and made a terrible face.

"Oh, God," he choked. "I don't think anyone would ever accidentally drink that!"

He held his nose, opened his mouth, and poured as much of the concoction down his throat as he could manage.

He held it down long enough to make it to his bed, where he laid down. He listened to the rushing river through his open front door.

An immensely strong convulsion started in his stomach and wrenched him this way and that. A moment later, his heart stopped. Ned Summers was dead.

Chapter Eighteen

Ned Summers opened his eyes just as Stanley Dill unleashed a powerful roundhouse punch, which connected flush with Ned's nose. Blood spurted everywhere and the boys who had formed a circle around them all took a half step back.

Stanley's eyes grew wide, as though he never actually expected the blow to land with such spectacular results. In a different kind of fight, he would have closed with a battering array of blows. But this was not that kind of fight.

Ned fought to open his watering eyes wide.

"Where am I?"

"Whoa, you really knocked old Summers for a loop," Jack Michaels said with a cackle. "He doesn't even know where he is."

Ned's eyes rolled back in his head and he collapsed in a heap on the ground.

"I think you killed him, Dill!"

Stanley Dill stood there with his hands dropped below his waist, uncertain of what to do. A powerful voice sounded beyond the boys. "What's going on here?" It was Gavin Temple, Middle Falls High School's principal, circa 1952.

He surveyed the scene, taking in Stanley's suddenly pale face and Ned's prone body.

"This is what happens when you boys roughhouse. Someone ends up getting hurt. Mr. Dill, you are to go to my office and wait for me there."

Stanley opened his mouth to object but then looked at Ned lying on the ground, still unconscious. He chose not to make an argument he knew he couldn't win.

The rest of the boys scattered like leaves on an autumn wind.

Temple kneeled down beside Ned and rearranged his arms and legs so he was lying somewhat more comfortably. As he did, Ned's eyes fluttered open.

"Good. Good. You're coming around. Just lay here for a minute. Then we'll go see the nurse and have you checked out."

Ned repeated the only words he had spoken since opening his eyes here. "Where am I?"

"Son. Ned. You're right outside the school. It looks like you and Stanley Dill were engaging in some fisticuffs." He reached out and turned Ned's face a bit to the left, examining his nose. "And it appears you got the worst of it."

Ned sat up, and blood poured out of his nose and down onto his shirt.

He looked Gavin Temple in the eye and said, "Mr. Temple? That's impossible. You've been dead for—well, I don't know how long, but I'm sure it's been a long time."

"I think you might have got hit harder than I had originally thought. Let's get you inside to see the nurse. Once she examines you, we might need to take you over to the hospital. If we do, we'll call the work number for your father."

"Father?" Ned said, rubbing his hand across his forehead. "Dad?"

"Yes, of course."

Ned jumped to his feet and said, "I'm gonna go."

"No, young man. You're not. We are going to see the nurse."

Ned nodded at him, but he still turned and walked away. After a few steps, he started to jog, and then he started to run.

Temple was so stunned at not being obeyed that he stood there with his mouth open, unsure of how to proceed. Ned ran right by the bike rack that held only one bicycle—his. He ran effortlessly as his young arms and legs propelled him forward.

What's happening? Is this all some fever-dream brought on by the hemlock? Am I still back in the cabin, slowly dying, while I dream I'm here?

He ran on, because the faster he ran, the less he had to think. Finally, a few blocks from his house, he was winded, so he slowed down. He bent over to catch his breath and he watched the blood spatter from his nose and onto the sidewalk. He touched his nose tenderly and he winced.

For a dream, this is damn realistic, because that hurts like hell.

He looked up at the trees, the blue skies, and the sunshine, listening to the birds nattering overhead.

In fact, I can never remember a dream that was anything like this. Is this what the afterlife is? Just a drop-in to various places in my life?

He hurried to what had been the house he shared with his mother and father once upon a time. Just like always, the back door was open. The house smelled exactly right—slightly stale, the smell of some fried meat from the night before still lingering in the air. He hadn't smelled it in close to fifty years, but he knew it was exactly right.

No dream could reproduce that.

He wandered through the house, letting his fingers lightly touch things—the door casing, the back of his father's chair, and the smooth surface of the kitchen table.

But if this is as real as it feels like it is, then I'm somehow back in Middle Falls in 1952. And...wait, I got into that fight with Stanley Dill the day before I went out with Mary Malone. Which means she's alive. And maybe she thinks we've got a date to keep tomorrow night. And if Mary's still alive, that means Dad is, too.

He stepped into the small bathroom and looked at his nose in the mirror. At first glance, it was a horror show—blood was drying at the corners, on his upper lip, and where it had dribbled down onto his shirt.

He picked a washcloth up off the tub and couldn't help but wonder if that was the same washcloth some other version of Ned Summers had used that very morning. Or, was it him who had used it, just in a different part of a time loop?

In any case, the washcloth felt real. He ran it under the tap and dabbed gently at his nose. Everywhere the blood had dried hurt like hell when he tried to clean it. With a little time, soap, water, and persistence, he was able to clean it all and rinse it down the drain. The same wasn't true for the shirt he was wearing. He took that off and went into his room to retrieve an old T-shirt, stuffing the bloody shirt deep under his bed.

When he went back in the bathroom and examined his nose once again, he decided it didn't look too bad. Yes, it was a little swollen, and there were still trace amounts of blood inside his nostrils that he wasn't brave enough to tackle but still, he was almost passable.

In a daze, he walked back into the kitchen and found the hamburger set out to thaw. He grabbed a few potatoes from the potato bin, chopped them up, and set them to fry with some bacon. He had the burgers on at a low heat when he heard the distinctive sound of his old Dodge pickup come into the driveway.

That would be Dad's *pickup, not mine, if this is 1952 after all.*

Ned's heart leaped into his throat. He hadn't seen his father in more than forty years. Was it really possible he was about to walk through the back door?

Chapter Nineteen

William Summers walked through the back door and set his battered lunchbox on the counter.

"Smells good!" he offered.

Ned could only marvel at him. Everything up to that moment was completely on point, but this was different. This was his father. This was the most important person in his entire life.

Without a thought, Ned threw his arms around his dad and hugged him. He immediately regretted it when he bumped his painful nose against William's shoulder and added to his watery eyes.

William accepted the embrace and patted his son's shoulder. When Ned let go, William had a surprised smile on his face, which faded a little when he saw Ned's nose. He touched Ned's cheek and moved his head right, then left, and then right again.

"Well, I don't think it's broken. Walk into a door at school today?"

Ned smiled as best he could, shrugging and saying, "Kind of."

"Well, I've run into a door or two myself over the course of my life. There's worse things in the world. Lemme go to the bathroom and clean up a little. Then we can eat."

Ned watched his father's back disappear around the corner and into the bathroom. He took two plates out of the dish rack on the counter and dished up their supper. By the time William emerged from the bathroom, Ned was already halfway done eating. The two of them were not much for standing on convention or manners.

Ned had several million things to think about, but that was one of the best things about his relationship with his father—they knew how to be quiet around each other.

What the hell do I do now? Is it a coincidence that I opened my eyes on this particular day, just before everything spun out of control? Doesn't seem like it. What are the odds that I am here, instead of waking up as an eight-year-old, or when I was already living out at the cabin?

William opened the front door and picked up that day's copy of *The Middle Falls Chronicle.* He settled into his old armchair and started to read.

Ned picked up the dishes and took them into the kitchen. While he filled the sink full of hot, soapy water, he did his best to make a plan.

What's best? To avoid Mary altogether tomorrow? Will that change her history so she's not killed? That seems like a cowardly thing to do—save myself and let her die.

He rinsed the plates and silverware, setting them back in the dish drainer to dry until tomorrow.

But I obviously don't want to do exactly what I did last time. That won't work. Maybe I could go out with Mary, but not come home and go to bed. I could park down the street and see who it was she snuck out to meet. That'll tell me who killed her last time. I can stop it from happening this time and things will be good again, right?

He wiped his hands on a dishrag that was sitting on the counter.

I need to face it. I don't understand anything about this at all. I don't really know where or when I am, how I got here, or what's best for me to do. But if this isn't just some fever-dream I'm having while I am dying in the cabin, I've got to just do the best I can.

Ned walked back into the living room and sat down on the couch. "Dad? Can I ask a favor?"

William lowered the paper. "Of course. What do you need?"

Ned took a deep breath. *This will commit me to a course of action.*

"Can I borrow your pickup tomorrow?"

William thought for a minute and then said, "Sure, I don't need it. Question is why do you need it?"

"I kind of have a date." Ned tried to catch himself from saying that, but it was too late. It already slipped out.

"That's not one of those things you kind of do. You've either got a date or you don't."

Déjà vu, Dad.

"You're right. I *do* have a date."

"Good for you. Who are you taking out?"

"Mary Malone."

If the name rang a bell with William, he didn't let on. He pulled his wallet out and offered two one-dollar bills to Ned. They had a remarkably similar tussle about whether Ned would take the money or not, but just as he had the first time, he ended up accepting them with gratitude.

Is life going to be this simple? This much the same? Can't be. Soon, I'll be making different decisions and meeting different people, and things will be different.

William returned to reading the sports page, but Ned could see that somehow the fact that he had a date had pleased his father. Ned went to his room, retrieved a book off his bookshelf, and returned to the couch—ostensibly to read, but instead, he just let his mind wander.

A second chance. A chance to fix the things that went wrong the first time. He let his mind recall his time in the cabin. He had lived simply, without running water, but surrounded by peace and beauty. *If I have a chance to do things differently this time, what do I do? I went to the cabin to get away from the whispers of town, but I need to be honest with myself. I could have come back almost any time after that. I stayed there because I wanted to.*

He stood up and stretched. "Gonna hit the hay, Dad. 'Night."

"See you tomorrow night, boy."

In his bedroom, Ned shucked off his clothes and slipped between the sheets. He lay on his back, his hands behind his head as he stared up at the ceiling. *No way I can go to sleep this early. Too much to think about.*

Two minutes later, he was asleep.

Chapter Twenty

When Ned's alarm went off at six-thirty the next morning, he sat straight up in bed, bleary-eyed and uncertain where he was. The familiarity of his room around him reminded him where—and when—he was.

A knot formed in his stomach. A jumble of thoughts tumbled through his mind all at once.

Will I be in trouble with Mr. Temple for running away from him yesterday? Do I care if I'm in trouble with Mr. Temple? Will my bike still be at school this morning? And what about Mary Malone? What do I do about her?

He realized he had no answers to any of those questions, so he poured himself a bowl of Wheaties, combed his hair, and set out for school.

A few blocks shy of the school, Stink Mitchell caught up to him.

"Hey, Summers! Wait up!"

It wasn't until that moment that Ned realized he had never seen Stink after he had moved out to the cabin. Not really at all after they had graduated, in fact.

I wonder what happened to you, Stink, you old boy.

When Stink caught up to him, the first thing he said was, "I heard you got knocked for a loop yesterday—that ole Dilly boy kind of cleaned your clock."

"I guess I forgot to duck," Ned said, quoting President Ronald Reagan after he had been—or, would be—shot some thirty years in the future or the past, depending on how you measured such things.

"We were never gonna get to college on a boxing scholarship anyway, were we?" Ned asked.

At school, two of his early-morning questions were answered. His bicycle was still sitting in the rack when he walked by it. Stink noticed it sitting there, but had the good grace not to ask why.

Ned felt his gut tighten when he walked back into school.

I don't remember where my locker is or what homework I might have had, and I don't care one bit. It's amazing what the perspective of an extra fifty years of living can do for you. At least I remember where homeroom was. Is. Whatever.

He went to his first class of the day and waited to see if Mr. Temple would track him down and drag him by the ear into his office. He didn't pay any attention to what was happening in class, and when everyone else turned in a homework assignment, he just didn't.

He walked into the hallway teeming with freshly brushed and scrubbed teenagers, but he felt very much apart from them.

I don't think I want to go to school any more today.

Ned casually walked to the front doors, went out into the warm morning sunshine, threw a leg over his bike, and pedaled away.

It's a beautiful day, I'm young and strong again, and I can go anywhere I want.

He rode randomly through a Middle Falls that he hadn't seen in decades.

But really, can *I go anywhere I want? Dad's alive again. Mary's alive, or at least I think she is, and I'm supposed to pick her up for a date tonight. And that's a little weird, too, isn't it? I'm an old man, and she's a young girl. Still, if I'm going to stop her from being killed, I'm going to have to go through with it.*

With time to kill, Ned rode his bike to Whitaker Park. He didn't have to worry about prying eyes spying on him, because on this day, there was nothing special about the park. It hadn't yet become the dumping ground for Mary Malone's body.

He laid his bike on its side in the familiar spot and scoped the area out. In a few years, there would be a housing development behind the park, but on this day, there were still acres of tall evergreens. At the edge of that forest was a greenbelt full of ferns, tall scrub grass, and blackberry bushes. Running alongside the greenbelt was the one-lane service road.

Ned walked along it, trying to remember exactly where Mary's body had been found. When he thought he had located it, he stepped off the distance between the road and that spot.

Thirty feet, give or take.

For the thousandth time, he tried to picture what had transpired here.

Did she come here to park with someone and they tried to push her too far? But how would that lead to someone shooting her? There's no motive for shooting her, no matter what, unless someone just wanted her dead. If so, though, why? Why would anyone want a twenty-year-old woman dead?

It was the same dead-end conversation he'd played through his brain so often when he'd been sitting alone on the riverbank by his cabin.

A new thought settled into his brain. *Is Mary really still alive? Maybe I'm making assumptions about things I shouldn't.*

On a whim, Ned rode his bike to Smith and Sons Grocery. He checked his wallet to make sure he actually had some money with him and he found the two dollars his father had given him the night before.

Inside the store, he glanced at the cash register but he saw that no one was there. Midday on a Friday was not the busiest of times at the little grocery.

He wandered to the vegetables and picked up a couple heads of corn on the cob, which were only two for a nickel. Back at the front of the store, Mary Malone, the woman of his dreams—as well as his nightmares, and the accidental source of a lifetime of heartache and headache—stood smiling at Ned.

"Well, Ned Summers. Aren't you the anxious one? Couldn't wait until tonight to see me?"

Ned tried to smile, but it felt numb and awkward on his face, so he lifted the corn on the cob as evidence of his true intentions.

Mary laughed a little, but she said, "Okay, then. Five cents, Mr. Summers."

Ned fished his wallet out and laid a dollar bill on the counter. Mary punched several buttons on the register. When she hit the large button, a red "Cash Sale" popped up in the small window facing the customer. As she made change, she said, "Shouldn't you still be in school?"

Truthfully, Ned said, "I didn't feel like going to school today."

"When I was still in school, there were many days I didn't feel like going, but my mama made sure I did anyway. Maybe you're more of a rebel than I thought you were."

Ned finally managed a goofy smile, and with a sudden panic, he realized he didn't remember what time he was supposed to pick her up. He remembered most things about that night, but it *had* been more than fifty years since it had originally transpired.

As casually as possible, he asked, "What time am I picking you up again?"

She narrowed her eyes at him, but then she decided he was joking. "You know what time. Seven o'clock, and don't be late or else mama won't let you in the door. She doesn't like tardy boys, and neither do I."

Chapter Twenty-One

The previous day and a half had been so weird as to be indescribable for Ned Summers, but he had handled it, for the most part, with aplomb. Well, he at least handled it better than most people who take the final leap into the abyss as an old man and instantly open their eyes on the wrong end of a punch to the nose.

He had seen his father and, for the most part, held it together. As he walked up the walkway to Mary Malone's front door, though, he started to lose it. His hands were so wet he made a mental note not to shake hands or touch anyone. His knees had an odd sensation of weakness in them, as if they had taken a separate vote and decided to go back home and go to bed. Unlike his first life, he hadn't bathed in Old Spice, so at least he didn't smell like a walking cologne factory.

He hesitated and took a deep breath before he knocked. Before his knuckles had a chance to connect, the door swung open slightly.

A young girl in pigtails and freckles stood at the door with a slightly evil smile on her face. She took some pleasure in Ned's obvious uncertainty.

"Mary, the victim of the day is here!" she shouted over her shoulder.

Mary Malone appeared around the corner with a smile. "Right on time, I see. Smart boy."

In his first life, when he had seen Mary dressed for their date, it had taken his breath away. She looked exactly the same on this night as she had then, but the effect was noticeably different. She seemed so young now. That wasn't surprising, though. To Ned's old man eyes, even his father, who was in his early fifties, had looked young to him. Everyone looked younger than the aged face he had grown used to looking at in the mirror.

From around the corner, a woman's voice said, "Mary, ask your young man to come inside so we can meet him."

Mary rolled her eyes a touch at Ned and then pushed her little sister out of the way so Ned could come inside. Ned walked into the center of the room, ready for the polite grilling he knew he was about to receive. Mr. Malone, hidden behind his copy of *The Middle Falls Chronicle*, didn't get up or even bother to look at Ned. He was as removed from the scene as he could be while still being in the same room.

Mrs. Malone emerged from the kitchen. She was wearing a dress and a white apron with frills on the edges. She held her hand out to Ned and said, "I'm Constance Malone."

Ned, who had furtively dried his hands on the back of his pants as he walked, shook it politely.

"Do I know your parents?"

"Probably not. My mom died a few years back, and my dad works in construction."

"Oh, I'm sorry," Constance Malone clucked at the news of Mrs. Summers' passing. "I didn't know."

"Tuberculosis."

Mrs. Malone's head nodded in a sympathetic angle. She then said, "Such a terrible disease. I think they've got it on the run now, but it has been terrible."

"And do you have a job yet?"

"I'm graduating next week from Middle Falls High."

At least I think I'm still graduating next week. Would they hold my diploma for skipping school today? Do I care?

"I've been working down at Coppen's Hardware this past year."

"Oh, that's nice. Mr. and Mrs. Coppen are part of our church."

Ned had no idea what to say to that so he let the conversation lapse.

Mary picked up the ball and ran with it. "Okay, well, we don't want to be late."

"What time does the movie get out?" Mrs. Malone asked, showing that her preliminary research was already done.

"Around nine-thirty," Ned said. "But then I thought we might go by Artie's and get a milkshake."

"Fine, fine. Just have Mary home by ten-fifteen, please."

Ned recognized that it wasn't a request, but rather an order.

"Yes, ma'am, I sure will. No problem."

"I'll leave the porch light on until you get home," Mrs. Malone said.

"I know, Mom," Mary said. She turned to Ned and raised her plucked eyebrows with a tight smile that said, "Quick! Let's escape while we can!"

"Nice meeting you," Ned said to Mr. and Mrs. Malone, even though he had never even seen Mr. Malone's face during the brief encounter.

Safely outside, Ned chuckled a little.

"That's the worst part of the night, I promise," Mary said.

"Ah, that wasn't so bad. They just worry about you. I understand."

Mary cast a sideways look at Ned. "You are an old man before your time."

"Right on schedule, actually," Ned replied as he opened the door of his father's truck for her.

Ned pulled away from the curb and drove to the Pickwick downtown. On the way there, they drove by Whitaker Park. His eyes automatically wandered to that spot, but Mary failed to notice.

"Do you know what *The Quiet Man* is about?" Ned asked.

"Oh, no. Why? Do you?"

"Uh-huh. John Wayne plays a boxer who ends up in Ireland. It's kind of a fish-out-of-water story."

"A fish-out-of-water story," Mary repeated. "I've never heard that before, but it's colorful. How do you know about the movie? It just started playing. Did you sneak off from school and see a matinee today?"

"No," Ned said with a small laugh. "I guess I must have read a review of it in the newspaper. I think it looks good, though. I'm glad we're going to see it."

"Maureen O'Hara is so beautiful. I wish I had red hair and her complexion," Mary said with a flip of her own dark curls.

Ned saw that as what it was—a chance to deliver a compliment—but he passed up the opportunity. Instead, he pulled into the Pickwick parking lot.

"Shall we?"

Chapter Twenty-Two

Inside the theater, Ned said, "Would you like something from the snack bar?"

"Are you going to get something?"

"I don't think so. I had dinner just before I left the house, and I want to leave room for a shake at Artie's. But you should get something."

"If you insist," she replied. "I'll have a Baby Ruth."

"How about a Coke to drink?"

Mary smiled as though he had read her mind. "Yes, please."

Ned waited in the small line, got her treat, and then took her elbow, leading her upstairs to the balcony. He found a spot a few rows back and right in the middle.

Mary made a small show of the way she ate her candy bar, just as she had the last time Ned had lived this scenario. Unlike the first time, when the process fascinated him, he just stared straight ahead, waiting for the film to start.

Surely this life will diverge from the one I already lived as time passes, won't it? I've already done many things different. Tonight, I plan to stop whoever killed Mary from doing it again. That would have to cause a major upset and everything will be completely different from then on, right? I don't want to live the same life a second time.

The newsreel and cartoon played, after which point *The Quiet Man* came on. Ned found it easy to lose himself in the movie. He hadn't seen it since his last life, more than fifty years ago, according to his way of thinking. In fact, *The Quiet Man* was the last movie he had ever seen. He did eventually get a generator for his cabin, but he never dreamed of bringing a television or a VCR there. He was happy with the entertainment the woods gave him every day.

When the movie was over, Ned stood up to leave and Mary hooked her arm through his as they descended the stairs.

It's funny. The last time we did this, all I thought about was how to impress you. This time around, I couldn't care less about that. And yet, the more I ignore you, the more you seem to like me. Is that just the way women are? No wonder I never was able to figure them out.

They drove to Artie's and parked in the lot. Ned turned in his seat. "Let me guess. You like chocolate?"

Mary seemed a bit surprised, but she recovered quickly. "Doesn't every girl?"

"Be right back," Ned said, hopping down out of the truck.

He looked around the little shack and marveled at how small it had become once more. He had never eaten at Artie's again in his last life, but it was the last thing he saw in Middle Falls on the way to his cabin, so he had watched it grow and change over the years. In just a few years, it will have quadrupled in size and taken over the empty lot next door, just for parking alone. Now, the Artie's that stood in front of him was almost nothing.

When he got to the front of the line, he saw the face of a boy whose name he had forgotten over the years.

"Hey, Ned, how you doing?" the young man said.

"Good, good."

"It's Zimm. Perry Zimmerman. Man! I can't believe you forgot me already. It's only been a couple of years."

For you, maybe.

"Hey, Perry. How you doin'? Can I get a couple of chocolate shakes?"

"Here on a date, huh? Good for you. Wish that's what I was doing, instead of frying burgers. I'll grab 'em for you. That'll be twenty cents."

Two minutes later, Ned was back in the truck. He handed the shake to Mary and said, "Guess who I saw? Perry Zimmerman. He must have gone to school with you. I think he graduated the same year you did."

Mary took a quick sip of her shake and smiled appreciatively. "Perry? Perry Zimmerman? Hmmm. I don't remember him."

"Huh. Maybe I'm wrong. No big deal."

Or maybe you just didn't pay attention to guys like Perry. I think that's more likely.

Ned glanced at his watch. "Almost ten o'clock. Maybe we better drink our shakes while we drive. I don't want to get you home late."

"I swear, I have never seen a boy so anxious to get rid of me. Do you have another date or something?"

"No," Ned laughed. "I just promised your mom I would have you home on time."

They drove home in silence, both of them doing their best to get to the bottom of their shakes before they got there. Mary won that particular race, after which she dabbed at her lips with a tissue from her purse and reapplied her lipstick, borrowing the rear-view mirror as she did so.

Ned pulled up to the curb in front of the Malone house, noting that the porch light was on, as expected.

Mary followed his eyes. "Yes, Mom is well-hidden behind those heavy draperies in the living room. She missed her calling when she didn't become a private eye. She's not quite as sharp as she thinks she is, though. I use soap on my window frame so I can open it real quiet-like and sneak out after she's gone to bed. She never knows."

Mary's eyes glowed with mischief.

"You never know," Ned cautioned, remembering that Mrs. Malone very much *did* know when she had snuck out.

"Well, even if she does, she never grounds me for it," Mary said with a shrug. "So it's all the same to me."

She looked at Ned with a wide-eyed innocence, edging imperceptibly closer to him and inviting a kiss.

Ned purposefully missed the signal.

"Don't sneak out tonight, okay? Just stay put."

"That is mighty presumptuous of you," she said, taken aback.

"I don't mean with me. I mean with anybody. Please just stay in your room tonight, okay?"

"I don't have any intention of doing anything else, thank you very much. What kind of girl do you think I am?"

"I think you're the kind of girl who just told me she puts soap on her window so she can sneak out at night."

"Why, I never!" Mary said. She slid across the seat, opened the car door, and disappeared up the walk in a huff.

Doubt that'll do the trick, but I had to try. Now, where shall I hide to wait?

Chapter Twenty-Three

Ned hadn't had a lot of time to plan his strategy for the night. He had spent much of the previous day-and-a-half wandering around in a daze, just trying to figure out what had happened and how he had gotten there. Now, with the crucial hours and minutes approaching, he had to make plans on the fly.

He reviewed the events of the night again and again. If he was honest with himself, he would have admitted that he had never *stopped* reviewing those events.

He sat for a minute, watching Mary retreat into her house. "Guess I don't have much of a future with her now, but any chance of a future for us didn't turn out so well last time, either," he said to himself.

He put the truck in gear, suddenly aware of how loud the muffler was in the quiet night air. He drove for two blocks, pulled a u-turn, and parked facing the other way. He got out of the truck and walked around it, craning his neck as he went. He couldn't see the Malone house from any angle.

Good enough.

He checked his watch. It was exactly ten-ten at night.

The problem is that I have no idea what the time frame is, or was, for the rest of the night. It's possible Mary went in the house and directly left through the window in her bedroom. Or she might have waited for hours until the whole household had gone to bed and then snuck out. Since her body wasn't discovered until almost two days later, I have no idea what the timeline is. Or was. This verb tense business is so complicated.

Ned stuck his hands in his pockets and casually walked up the sidewalk on the side of the street opposite Mary's house. He slowed down as he neared her family's home. He felt exposed and naked, just creeping through the neighborhood.

Wouldn't that be great, though, if someone called the cops on me for being a peeping Tom?

When he saw the corner of Mary's house, he crossed the street and did his best to melt into a line of bushes that ran between the Malones' home and their neighbor's house. He squirmed around a bit, and even though branches were sticking him in his ribs, he had a good view of the Malone house.

Just the front of the house, though. What good is that going to do me? Mary's room is in the back. When she sneaks out, does she go around the back, or does she come to the front?

He pushed through the rough tangle of limbs and leaves as he worked his way toward the back of the house. He finally made it to the point where he could lean forward and peek around to the back of the house, but that was precisely when a dog next door began to bark.

And bark.

And bark.

Loud and long.

The dog had caught scent of Ned and didn't like him prowling around one bit. Ned looked over his shoulder, praying that he wouldn't see a huge German Shepherd inches away from him. Ned only saw a tall fence, but the dog was definitely making itself known by scratching at the wooden slats and barking endlessly.

Above the din of the dog, a door opened and a gruff voice said, "Brutus. Brutus! Knock it off."

Brutus. Of course. The house next door couldn't keep small dogs, like a Chihuahua. No, it has to be some big, slobbering monster named Brutus.

Brutus did not knock it off. If anything, the urgency in his barks increased.

"Whatsamatter boy? Something out there? If it's a skunk, leave it alone. If it's a prowler, chew their balls off."

As quietly as possible, Ned stepped out from the hedge and ran alongside it, hoping he was still deep enough in the shadows so no one would spot him. Behind him, Brutus continued to contribute to the neighborhood watch.

Once he started running, Ned had a hard time stopping. He flew up the sidewalk until his Dad's old truck was in sight. A few moments later, he was back inside, his adrenaline running high and his heart hammering.

He sat behind the wheel of the truck until his breathing returned to normal.

What now? Try the other side of the house? I don't think that'll go any better than this one did. I am not cut out to be a cat burglar.

He nervously tapped his hand against the truck's steering wheel. Each second that passed only heightened the levels of tension and pressure that he felt.

If I'd known I would actually get a chance to live this whole damned thing over again, I would have made a plan. Instead, I'm running around blind. So, if I can't stop her as she's coming out of her window, what can I do?

Ned started the truck and let it idle noisily.

The only other thing I know for sure is that she was killed over at the park. I can head over there and stop it before it happens. It ain't much of a plan, but it's all I've got. For your sake, Mary, I hope this works.

Ned drove through the silent streets. Middle Falls didn't actually roll up the sidewalks after ten at night but it might as well have. As he turned right toward Whitaker Park, he finally saw another vehicle. It was a Middle Falls police car. The car was coming from the other direction, but it turned onto the same street Ned was on. As it passed him, a streetlight illuminated both drivers.

Ned saw Chief Deakins.

Chief Deakins saw Ned.

It was too late to duck or hide, so Ned elected to just look like he had all the right in the world to be sitting there. Which he did, of course. There was no curfew and no law against driving the streets.

Of course, if I don't stop Mary from being murdered, the fact that Deakins saw me will be one more piece of evidence to use against me. I can just picture him interrogating me. "What were you doing in Mary's neighborhood so long after you dropped her off? What were you doing exactly?"

Ned turned right and motored toward Whitaker Park.

Chapter Twenty-Four

The service road that ran along the side of the park wasn't much. It wasn't paved, and it was more like two worn tire tracks, with grass growing up between them.

Ned turned onto the service road and drove slowly along the grove of trees. The night was clear, but it was a new moon, so it was inky black. The headlights lit up the grass in sharp relief. As he approached the area where Mary's body was found, his stomach knotted.

"What's best? What's best?" Ned wondered to himself.

Should I park right here, where her body was found, so I can stop her from being killed? Or will they see my truck and take her somewhere else to do it? I think that's more likely. If they do that, I might never even see them.

The service road made a complete loop around the park, passing garbage cans, a playground swing set, and picnic tables. Eventually, Ned emerged onto the same road he had been on before. He drove a block away and parked.

It was a warmish night, but in Western Oregon, that can change. Ned didn't know how long he was going to be waiting for a killer, so he grabbed the jacket he had stuffed behind the seat.

He leaned over, opened the glove box, and took out the .22 handgun that belonged to his father. He tucked it into his jacket pocket, locked up the truck, and walked back to the park.

Five minutes later, he was standing at what had once been, and could be once more, the scene of one of Middle Falls' most famous murders. He turned all the way around. There was no sign of life, not to mention a sign of light, considering that the park didn't have street lights installed until 1958.

Ned squinted at this watch. It was still only eleven-thirty.

I could be here all night. Might as well get comfortable.

He stepped off the service road and walked directly to the spot where Mary's body had been found. He put his hands into his jacket pocket and found the touch of the .22-caliber gun very comforting. He took a few more steps into the underbrush and found a tree to lean against.

As the minutes passed, he sat on his haunches.

Should have brought a flashlight with me.

His eyes were as adjusted to the dark as they could be, and he swept the area around the tree with his shoe. Once he found a decent spot, he sat down. It was too dark to be able to read his watch, so he had no idea what time it was.

The frogs and crickets that lived in the area eventually forgot he was there and serenaded him in a mighty chorus that made him homesick for his cabin.

Before he knew it, he had drifted off.

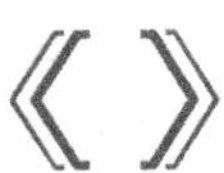

HEADLIGHTS PLAYED ACROSS Ned's face. His eyes flew open and he was completely blinded by the unexpected light. He threw up an arm to block the light, but still, all he could see were explosions of light and an after-image of the headlights danced in front of him.

He closed his eyes and cursed himself under his breath. He looked away and opened his eyes again, praying for them to adjust.

He heard the vehicle roll to a stop not too far away from where he sat. As quietly as possible, he stood up and moved behind the tree.

More than he had ever wanted anything in his life, he wanted to see who was at the murder spot with Mary.

Slowly, he peeked his head around the trunk of the tree. He squeezed his eyes shut, trying to get as much of his night vision back as possible.

Ned had spent many hours spread over many years trying to answer one question: who had come to this lonely spot with Mary? He had considered many suspects. Older boys with souped-up cars. Maybe even an older man she had seen, meeting her there in their family sedan.

Nothing he had imagined could prepare him for reality. What he saw, when his eyes finally cleared, was far beyond his wildest imagination.

Not more than forty feet away from him was the same Middle Falls police car he had seen on his way to the park.

What the hell? Is Chief Deakins tracking me somehow? How would he ever know I was here?

The squad car's headlights clicked off and darkness returned. The car sat there, quietly idling. Ned couldn't move. This was too much new information to take in at one time and his mind was frozen.

The driver's door opened and Chief Deakins, tall and strong, emerged. Unlike Ned, he had remembered to bring a flashlight. He switched it on and began crisscrossing a path in front of him.

Ned faded a little further behind the tree, trying to blend in with the surrounding foliage. If someone had asked Ned why he was afraid of being discovered there, he wouldn't have been able to answer, but he undoubtedly was frightened beyond measure.

The chief walked directly toward Ned, swinging the flashlight back and forth like a metal detector looking for lost coins. He stopped about fifteen feet away from Ned. Deakins held the flashlight steadily against a bare plot of land that was surrounded on all sides by brush and trees.

He flipped the flashlight off and walked briskly back to the prowler. He opened the trunk and bent over.

A moment later, he backed out of the seat, this time carrying something. He stood straight and walked unerringly back to the same spot he had been a moment before. Without any ceremony, he placed what he was carrying on the ground. Ned heard the crinkling of plastic as if something was being unrolled. A moment later, Deakins turned on his heel, and strode back to his car.

Before Ned could even gather his wits, Deakins was back in his car, continuing on the loop. One minute later, he had turned back on the street and his taillights disappeared down the road.

Ned ran to the spot. He had been hiding behind the tree and unable to see what Deakins had dropped, but he had a horrible idea what it was.

He managed to slow down amid the darkness just before tripping over Mary Malone's body.

Chapter Twenty-Five

Ned stopped dead. It was still pitch black, but there was something about the form in front of him—the way it unfolded on the ground beneath it—that eradicated any doubts in Ned's mind about what it was.

His legs went out from under him and he sat down with a *thump*. When he did, his knee touched Mary's side. He reached out his hand and tentatively touched her. Her body was still warm and pliable. When he drew his hand back, it was sticky, but he didn't need to wonder what caused it.

"Goddamn it!" Ned shouted into the sky, not caring who might hear him. Then, softly to Mary, he whispered, "Goddamn it. I tried to save you."

The evidence—a shadowy pile of humanity merely inches away—spoke of his failure. For the first time in more years than he could remember, Ned felt tears forming. He let them come. There was no reason to hold them back. He let himself be taken over by sobs for Mary. For his messed-up life that he didn't understand. For just about everything, really.

He eventually gained control of himself with a few deep, shuddering breaths.

And now what do I do? What is *there to do? Nothing, right? I am right back where I was in my last life. What is there to do but to see it through?*

An image of his cabin in winter formed in his mind. He could see snow forming an insulating layer over his roof, a fire burning hot in his woodstove, and a pot of coffee sitting on top. The image restored and fortified him.

I'm sorry, Mary. I thought I was saving you, but I was just bumbling around. The best I can do now is get away and let things run their course.

He stood up, dusted off the seat of his pants, and looked up into the dark night sky.

One thought, and one thought alone, filled his mind.

Deakins was here.

He stepped gently over what had been Mary Malone just a few hours earlier. Ned strode toward his father's truck.

I will not let you get away with this. You and that asshole kept me in that little room, trying to break me until I almost did. I mean, I would have if Dad hadn't come in and saved me. And it was you the whole time. That's not okay. I can't save Mary, but I can bring you down.

NED WOKE UP THE NEXT morning and found his father drinking coffee at the table. When Ned came out of his bedroom, William made a show of looking at his watch.

"I thought I was going to have to wake you up to get you down to the hardware store in time for your shift. Must have been quite the date."

Hardware store. Coppen's Hardware Store. That's right. He didn't fire me until later in the summer, after everyone was already convinced I had killed Mary.

"You better grab a bowl of cereal. Old man Coppen will work you within an inch of your life, just like always does. It's good for you, but you don't want to go on an empty stomach."

Ned couldn't summon his words yet, so he just nodded and went into the kitchen to pour himself some cereal and milk. As he carried his bowl to the table, William passed him as he headed out the back door.

"See you tonight. I'll be home first, so I'll make dinner."

"Okay, Dad. Sounds good."

It was so good to see his father alive and healthy again, but it was hard for Ned to take any pleasure in that, or anything at all, really. The black cloud of failing to save Mary had settled over him and anger seeped into his bones.

He finished his cereal, hopped on his bike, and pedaled to the hardware store. As predicted, Mr. Coppen had left him a long list of heavy labor on the chalkboard by the back door.

When Ned saw Mr. Coppen for the first time, he almost jumped in surprise. Old man Coppen was substantially younger than Ned had been just a few days earlier, prior to being reborn. Coppen looked like he might be in his late fifties.

It's all about perspective. He looked ancient to me when I was eighteen.

Ned put his nose to the grindstone and knocked off the entire list by three o'clock. Mr. Coppen examined his work, saying, "Good enough, Ned. Good enough. See you next Saturday."

Ned took his time riding home. He pedaled around town, letting the wind run over his face and his thoughts follow each other round and round in his head. He avoided Whitaker Park, of course, where he knew Mary Malone's body was, lonely and awaiting discovery.

Ned had considered calling in an anonymous tip to the police that would tell them where she could be found, but he decided not to risk it. What's done was done.

Instead, Ned made his plans for how he would manage to pin the murder on Deakins. He knew he couldn't just call up one of the deputies and say, "Hey, I know Chief Deakins killed Mary Malone." That would get him nowhere and only shine the spotlight on him.

Since Deakins was the law in Middle Falls, Ned knew he would have to go farther afield to recruit help. He knew that kind of help wouldn't be available on a weekend, and regardless, he had to wait until the discovery of Mary's body.

That made the rest of the weekend interminable. He felt like he was stuck in a bad dream, where nothing he did had any impact, and he was doomed to repeat mistakes he had already made.

On Sunday afternoon, as Ned was doing nothing more than sitting on the couch and reading a book, there was a knock on the door. Ned glanced out the window and saw the Middle Falls police car sitting in front of the house.

Shit. I forgot Deakins came by to question me before Mary was even discovered. Of course he did. If anyone knew a crime had been committed, it was him. He was already looking for some sucker to pin it on.

William was still gone, so Ned pushed off the couch and opened the door.

"Ned Summers?" Deakins asked, with a friendly expression on his face that said, *Sorry to bother you on the Sabbath.*

Ned nodded.

"Do you mind if I come in? I have a few questions I'd like to ask you."

"You know," Ned answered. "I think I do mind, Chief Deakins."

Chapter Twenty-Six

The fixed expression on Chief Deakins' face faded into one of confusion.

Ned began to close the door, but Deakins reached out and held it open. It wasn't quite like a pushy door-to-door salesman sticking his foot in the door, but it was in the same area code.

"I think you misunderstood me. You're not in trouble. I'm just investigating a missing person case that got called into me today and I need to talk with you about it."

Ned examined Deakins face closely.

Missing person case, huh? How can you manage to keep a straight face, when you were hauling that missing person *around in your trunk last night?*

Ned let up on closing the door, but he also didn't let it open any further. "What do you need to know?"

Deakins cocked his head to the right, seemingly puzzled by this reaction.

"If you don't want me to come inside, why don't you step out here on the porch so we can talk."

Ned shrugged, opened the door slightly, and stepped onto the porch.

Their conversation went much like it had in Ned's first life, with Deakins probing into the Friday night date—where they had gone, what they had seen, and what time he had dropped Mary off at her home.

When those details were covered and jotted down in Deakins' notebook, he said, "What did you do after you dropped Mary off?"

I hid in the bushes and watched you dispose of her body, you son of a bitch.

"I came home and went to bed."

"Did anyone see you when you came home?"

"No. My dad sleeps soundly. He wouldn't have heard me."

"I see." Deakins shut the notebook and slipped it into his shirt pocket. "When I spoke to Mrs. Malone, she told me that Mary had a habit of slipping out of her bedroom window after everyone else had gone to bed. Did she slip back out to see you on Friday night?"

If she slipped out to see anyone, it was you, and you killed her for it.

"No. As I just told you, I came straight home after I dropped her off."

"I know you did, and I appreciate that, but I had to ask. It's possible you were trying to avoid getting her in trouble or protecting her reputation."

Ned stared straight ahead. Since he was six inches shorter than Deakins, that put him at eye level with the chief's heavy, silver badge.

"Anything else, Chief?"

Deakins took a step off the small porch, so he looked Ned right in the eye. Ned didn't look away. "I think that's all I need," Deakins said.

Ned went inside and closed the door behind him.

Ned decided against going to school that week. He just couldn't face the idea of being in that environment and not remembering anyone or anything. At the same time, he made the strategic decision not to tell his father, as he knew the result of that would be exceptionally negative.

William Summers left for work early, so as long as Ned was up and appearing like he was going to school, his dad was none the wiser.

The only telephone in the house was attached to the wall in the kitchen. The thin Middle Falls phone directory didn't have the number he wanted. Stuck at the very back of a cabinet, he found a five-year-old Polk County directory, though. It wasn't likely that the number he needed would have changed, so Ned took a deep breath, said, "Sorry for the long-distance call, Dad," and dialed a Portland number.

A woman's voice on the other end of the line answered, saying, "Oregon Bureau of Investigation, Field Office. May I help you?"

NED HAD DONE HIS BEST to piece together how things had played out in the immediate aftermath of Mary's murder and the discovery of her body, including that Deakins had come and taken Ned out of class that Monday afternoon.

He expected the same thing this would happen time around, but of course, Ned wasn't in school so he couldn't be found there. Ned pulled the curtains, turned off all the lights, and sat in the semi-darkness, waiting.

He wasn't disappointed. Long before his dad was due home, he heard a car pull into their driveway, and then footsteps resounded against the porch steps, and a stern knock-knock pounded on the front door.

Ned didn't have any interest in talking to Deakins today. He had just called and turned him in to the Oregon Bureau of Investigation that morning, so Ned sat silently in a chair in the corner of the living room and waited.

Deakins knocked again and again. Eventually, Ned could hear him talking to someone. It was likely Mr. Randolph, who was attracted to people being outside the way a cat is attracted to a ray of sunshine on the floor. Ned couldn't quite hear the conversation through the door without moving closer, but he had no intention of walking through the creaky house and alerting Deakins to his presence. Besides, he could imagine what the conversation was like.

Ned waited patiently as he heard the buzz of voices back and forth for a few minutes.

Feel free to interrogate Mr. Randolph all you like. All he knows is that I'm a good kid who lives with my dad and mows the lawn on Sundays.

Eventually, the voices stopped, but Deakins came back and knocked on the door again for several minutes.

This is an eight-hundred-square-foot house. How long do you think it would take me to get to the door?

Finally, footsteps echoed down the steps, after which there were the sounds of a car door shutting and an engine starting. Ned heard the sound of the car turning onto the street and driving away. And still, he waited. He waited until the clock on the wall read four-forty-five, and then he got up and started dinner.

Just before five, Ned went to the window and threw the curtains open wide. In his heart of hearts, he believed Deakins would be standing with his boots in his mother's abandoned flower bed, grinning triumphantly.

Instead, it was just the yard, the street, and the late afternoon sunshine filtering through the leaves of the trees.

THE DAY BEFORE, NED had phoned the Oregon Bureau of Investigation and not only reported that the Middle Falls Police Chief had committed a murder, but that Ned had witnessed it. The agent he had spoken with seemed to have taken it quite seriously. He had asked a number of probing questions and seemed satisfied with the answers he received.

Finally, he had said, "I'm tied up all day today, but I've got time in my schedule tomorrow. If I come up in the late morning, where will you be? Can we meet?" he had asked.

Ned had quickly agreed to meet him at his house.

Now that it was already later into Tuesday morning, Ned anxiously sat on the couch, nervously awaiting the arrival of Agent Hankins from the OBI. Finally, just when he was about to give up and make himself a peanut butter and jelly sandwich for lunch, a sleek, four-door Ford sedan rolled up the street and turned into his driveway.

A tall, thin man in a gray suit stepped out of the car and put his hat on.

Looks like an OBI guy, no doubt.

Ned stood at the door waiting. As soon as the man knocked, Ned swung the door open as wide as he could.

"Good morning. I'm Agent Hankins, OBI." The man reached inside his suit jacket and withdrew a black wallet. He flipped it open and showed Ned a shiny gold badge, which read "Oregon Bureau of Investigation" around the outside. "Are you Ned Summers?"

"I am. I spoke to you on the phone yesterday."

"I thought you were older when I talked to you."

"I didn't think you'd come if you knew how old I am. It doesn't change what I saw."

"I suppose it doesn't."

"What do we do now?"

A sudden shadow loomed in the front door. Ned looked behind Hankins to see Chief Deakins.

"What happens now," Deakins said, "is that we arrest you for the murder of Mary Malone." He held his hand out, handcuffs dangling. "Turn around, please, and put your hands behind your back."

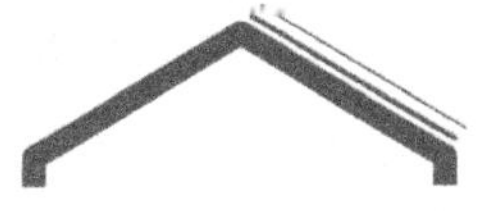

Chapter Twenty-Seven

Ned Summers sat in a small holding room in the Polk County Jail in Dallas, Oregon. Not to be confused with *The Dalles*, a bigger town further east, and definitely not to be confused with Dallas, Texas.

Dallas, Oregon, is no bigger than Middle Falls, Oregon, but Dallas is the county seat of Polk County. That means Dallas has the county jail, along with the few other official buildings of Polk County, including the county courthouse.

Ned couldn't be kept in Middle Falls because the jail is just two cells at the back of the police station, and they are really only used to let drunk and disorderly cases dry out before they get sent home. For a charge as serious as murder, something more long-term was required.

That afternoon, Deakins had put the cuffs on Ned and then Ned was put in the backseat of Agent Hankins' car. He was transported up to Dallas, where he was going to be held until the arraignment and likely trial. Deakins had wanted to take him in his own patrol car, but Hankins had said it was better if he took him in, given the circumstances.

And now, Ned sat in a windowless room in the not-too-big Polk County jail. He had been assigned a cell, but before he could even see what it looked like, a jailer had escorted him to this room and told him he had a visitor coming.

Ned sat with his arms resting on the table and his head resting on his arms.

I thought I could fix everything. Instead, I've messed up everything. I didn't save Mary, and now I'm worse off than I was in my last life. At least then I was free, and I had the forest and the river. Now I've got a six-by-eight cell and one hour of outside time every day—if I'm lucky.

The steel door swung open and Ned looked up to see a uniformed jailer with a set of keys in his hand. Behind him was William Summers.

Not gonna be so easy this time, Dad. You can't save me from myself like you did last time.

The jailer nodded at William and said, "Go ahead. Knock on the door when you're ready to go, or if you need something."

In movies, jailers and guards were all so surly and looking for their opportunity to hold their power over whoever crossed their paths. In this case, the man with the keys was kind and understanding. Clichés so often prove to be false.

William stepped inside and stood on the other side of the table. Ned stood up and realized that his face was wet with tears. He hadn't been aware that he had been crying.

"Sit down, son. We need to talk."

Ned ran his arm across his face, took a deep breath, and nodded. Father and son sat across from each other, staring into each other's eyes. Finally, William said, "I still see my son in those eyes. I wasn't sure if I would. Okay, then. I just need to ask you one question. Did you do this thing?"

Ned held his father's eyes with his gaze, and in a quiet voice, Ned said, "No."

William held Ned's eyes for a beat longer, after which he said, "That's all I needed to know. I'll go to bat for you, then."

"I don't want you to."

"What do you mean?"

"I mean, I want you to believe in me, and I want you to come see me whenever you want to, but I don't want you to do anything drastic, like take another mortgage out on the house or cash in your life insurance policy, just to pay for a lawyer for me."

That set William back. "How do you know about my life insurance policy?"

Because I know a lot of things an eighteen-year-old kid shouldn't know. And none of the things I know does me any good at all.

"That's the thing, Dad. There are a lot of things I know that I can't explain how I know. Like, I know you've either already bought me a pocket knife for my graduation, or you're planning on it. Like I know you took out this life insurance policy right after Mom died, so I'd be taken care of."

"I know you, boy. You're not the kind to go sneaking through my things. We've always respected each other's privacy."

"I know, Dad, and I still do. If I tried to tell you how I know these things, you'd think I'm completely crazy. I'll just tell you right now that I didn't hurt Mary. I would never, ever do something like that. I think they're going to be able to make it look like I did, though, so I'll probably be found guilty and have to go to prison. It stinks, but there's nothing I can do about it. You can ask me to explain a million times, but I just can't do it."

William didn't take a sweeping statement like that at face value. He poked, he prodded, and he asked the same question—*how do you know these things*—in a dozen different ways, but it was all to no avail.

"There are some things that are going to come out at trial, and I'll always be honest with you about them, but you probably won't like some of the truths you hear."

"Like what?"

"Like the fact that I took your .22 with me on the night Mary was killed."

Complete surprise registered on William's face. "What? Why in the world would you do that?"

"That's another one of those questions I can't really answer. And they will find that Mary was killed with a .22 as well."

William blanched.

Ned shook his head. "Don't worry, Dad. They can do ballistics testing on the bullets they retrieve from Mary and they will find it doesn't match up with your gun. And the reason for the lack of evidence is that I didn't shoot her, of course."

"What else?"

Ned dropped his eyes to the gray surface of the table.

"I was at Whitaker Park on Friday and I saw Chief Deakins take Mary's body out of the trunk of his police car and drop it in the woods."

That was too much for William. "Ned. Come on. Now you're making no sense. Why would our police chief kill someone, and how in the world would you know where to be when he did that? It's impossible."

"Sure seems that way, doesn't it? I told you there were some hard things you were going to hear, and I just wanted you to hear them from me. The best way you can help me is to stand with me. I'll put up the best defense I can. I don't want to go to prison. But I can do that with the assistance of a public defender. I don't want you to go in hock just to hire another attorney. I don't think it will make a difference anyway."

"There's so much here that I don't understand. You sound completely different. You're my son, but in another way, you're...not." William's eyes swept across Ned. "I'll tell you this, though. I'll be with you every step of the way. I'll never leave you."

Chapter Twenty-Eight

Ned Summers' trial was held less than a month later at the county courthouse in Dallas. Justice didn't drag her feet in 1952.

Ned ended up prevailing on his father and was represented by a public defender by the name of Chad Garr. Mr. Garr was a recent graduate of law school, and acting as the legal representation for Ned was not just Garr's first murder case, but his first case of any kind at all.

William Summers balked again when he met Mr. Garr, saying, "I've got socks older than that guy." The truth was that he actually did.

Nonetheless, Ned liked Garr, and they did well together for the most part, although they did come to loggerheads on certain issues.

A week before the trial, Allen King, the District Attorney for Polk County, approached Garr with a plea-bargain deal. He laid out the evidence against Ned, which was substantial, and then he offered the deal. If Ned were to plead guilty to second-degree murder, then King would recommend a thirty-year sentence. With good behavior, Ned could be out by his fortieth birthday. If he didn't accept the offer and the jury found him guilty of murder in the first degree, the D.A. would ask for the death penalty.

Being sent to the gas chamber didn't hold quite the same fear for Ned Summers as it did for most people. He had already visited the great beyond and it looked a lot like Middle Falls, Oregon, circa 1952.

What swung it for Ned, though, was that he couldn't bring himself to plead guilty to something he hadn't done. He turned the deal down. And so, after everyone who wasn't in jail enjoyed a nice three-day

Fourth of July weekend, the trial of Ned Summers started at nine in the morning, sharp, in Dallas, Oregon.

The Polk County courthouse wasn't large, but it had been built before the war ended and it was impressive for its size. It was also quaint with its marble floors and polished wood, along with the smell of an extensive law library.

The courtroom itself was not built to accommodate large crowds, but there were still six double rows of benches. At the front of the room, on a raised dais, was a tall desk. Behind that, the flag of the United States and the state flag of Oregon both hung limply on flag stands.

There was a good-sized crowd in attendance. William Summers was there, of course, as were Mary Malone's parents, anxious to see justice play out. Beyond them, the courtroom was filled with more viewers than normal. Many of the gawking spectators were people who had made the forty-minute drive from Middle Falls. There hadn't been a murder trial in Polk County in more than five years, so there was a lot of pent-up desire for the spectacle. The trial of Ned Summers more than sated the curious.

Seating the jury took less than an hour. Each side used only one of their challenges, and in short order, twelve of Ned's peers took their place in the jury box. Most looked pleased to have a seat of honor in the proceedings. The exception was Fin Abergast, a farmer from Dallas who insisted it was a hardship on his family to have him away during haying season.

Judge Merrick sympathized with him, though he seated him anyway. Fin could be heard muttering about how the judge would be up for reelection in two years.

Allen King made a persuasive opening statement, listing all the evidence, both direct and circumstantial, that they would present to the jury. He was painting the picture of Ned as a rejected suitor who snuffed out the life of the effervescent Mary Malone.

Every time King referred to the victim, Mrs. Malone could be heard sniffing and sobbing in the gallery.

Ned sat calmly beside his attorney, listening to the opening statement.

I know I'm innocent, but after hearing the case he laid out, I'd likely find myself guilty. Not sure what chance we've got of convincing anyone else.

Mr. King spent the rest of the day slowly closing the vice on Ned. He started by telling the story of Mary Malone's last day, most of which was not in dispute of either side. He wanted to establish what a good, normal, young woman Mary was. She had worked the day shift at Smith and Sons Grocery. Then, she went home, freshened up, and met Ned at her house for their date. They went first to the Pickwick to see *The Quiet Man*, then to Artie's for chocolate shakes. Finally, Ned dropped her off at home at ten in the evening.

Mrs. Malone was called to the stand and she testified that Mary seemed fine when she came in from her date, perhaps just a little nervous, if anything.

"A mother knows these things," she had said, dabbing at her eyes as she recalled the memory.

"What did your daughter do when she got home?"

"It was late for our family," Mrs. Malone answered. "We're early risers, so both Mary and I went to bed. My husband and other daughter were already asleep."

Mr. King asked for permission to approach the witness, which the judge granted.

"I'm sorry to have to probe some of these areas, but it's necessary to get at the truth of the matter," King explained.

"I understand," Mrs. Malone said, setting her chin firmly.

"Was Mary the type of girl who might sneak out of the house when everyone else was asleep?"

"Mary was a free spirit," Mrs. Malone said before tears sprang to her eyes once again. "I'm sorry. It's so hard to think of her in the past tense. To know that we will never see her again."

"Of course," King said, handing her a clean, white handkerchief. "So, you say she was a free spirit. Can I consider that a 'yes' to the question of whether she ever snuck out of the house?"

Mrs. Malone didn't answer, but instead, she simply nodded, causing the tears to spill down her cheeks.

"Let the record reflect that Mrs. Malone answered in the affirmative. That's all the questions I have for you, ma'am."

"Does the defense have any questions for this witness?" Judge Merrick asked.

Chad Garr flipped through his notes. He then stood and said, "No, your honor."

Having effectively established that Mary had likely voluntarily snuck out of her room that night, King focused his attention on Ned. He called Mr. Mitchem, the Malones' neighbor, to the stand. He testified that on the night of Mary's disappearance, his dog had gone crazy from barking, as if there was a stranger prowling the area.

In cross-examination, Garr asked how often his dog barked at things like squirrels, raccoons, and other creatures that go bump in the night. Mr. Mitchem admitted that it was not an unusual occurrence.

The next testimony was more damning. It came from Elouise Lampson, who owned a house just down the street from the Malones. She testified that on the night in question, she had been awakened from a sound sleep by a noisy muffler rattling in front of her house. When she looked outside, she saw a pickup truck sitting at the curb.

Mr. King produced a picture of William Summers' truck. "Was this the truck you saw?"

"It certainly appears to be," Mrs. Lampson replied.

Again, the defense had no questions for the witness. Young Mr. Garr was not the type to stand at the back of the courtroom and ask

Mrs. Lampson how many fingers he was holding up in an attempt to discredit her. He had been taught in law school to not ask a question he didn't already know the answer to.

Next up was Agent Hankins from the Oregon Bureau of Investigation. The District Attorney spent a few minutes establishing Hankins' bona fides, including twelve years as an OBI agent. He then asked Hankins to recount a phone call he had received from Ned Summers on Monday, May twenty-sixth.

"Mr. Summers told me that he had witnessed a crime. Specifically, he saw the dumping of a body in a city park."

"And did he say he knew who had committed this crime?"

"He did. He said it was Michael Deakins, the Middle Falls Police Chief."

That bit of testimony had not been public knowledge and it caused a twitter of conversation to ripple through the courtroom.

Judge Merrick banged his gavel and said, "Quiet please," but he didn't sound too stern. Bombshell testimony always elicited some reaction.

"What did you do next, Agent Harkins?"

"I asked him for more details, and he provided them, saying that Chief Deakins had the body wrapped in a piece of plastic in the trunk of his squad car, and that he had simply dropped the body onto the ground and then drove away."

"Did you ask Mr. Summers just how he came to be in a position to witness this?"

"I did. He was evasive, insisting that he had just been passing by."

"Uh-huh. Just passing by a deserted city park at what time?"

"He said it was after midnight."

"And what did you do with this information?"

"That's a pretty unusual phone call, so I took it up to my supervisor. We looked at it from all angles and figured that there were enough holes in the story that we needed to bring Chief Deakins in on the situation. I drove to Middle Falls, spoke to the Chief, and asked if he minded if I looked inside the trunk of his car."

"Did he cooperate?"

"Yes, sir. He took me straight to his squad car and opened the trunk. He also let me look around as much as I wanted."

"And what did you find?"

"The typical inside of a squad car trunk. Flares, a jack to help people change tires, an emergency first aid kit, and not much more."

"Did you detect any blood?"

"No, sir. None at all. From there, we assumed that the phone call had been a poorly conceived effort to pin the blame on another party and so we investigated it as such. We arrested the suspect, Mr. Summers, the next day."

On cross-examination, Garr asked if they had considered the possibility that Chief Deakins might know more than what he was saying.

Hankins shrugged. "Not after we looked at the evidence, no."

The prosecution's final witness was Terry Reynolds, the head of the Polk County crime lab. He testified that the gun the police had retrieved from the Summers household was indeed a .22—the same caliber weapon used to kill Mary Malone. He testified that the ballistics on the bullet showed that it was not the gun that was used in the murder.

Much more damaging was the pair of pants Ned had worn on that night. They had been recovered after Chief Deakins obtained a warrant to search the entirety of Summers' home. King held up the pants dramatically in front of the jury box, walking by them slowly, pointing to a stained area on the right knee of the pants.

"Mr. Reynolds, did the crime lab test this stain?"

"Yes, sir. It is blood."

"Was there enough blood to be able to test for the type?"

"Yes, sir. The blood we pulled from those pants was A-B negative."

"Is that a common blood type?"

"No, actually. It's quite rare. Less than one percent of the population has blood that is A-B negative."

"Can you tell me what Mr. Summers' blood type is?"

"A-positive."

"And Miss Malone's blood type?"

"A-B negative."

Chapter Twenty-Nine

At the moment of Mr. Reynolds' pronouncement, Ned happened to be looking at the jury. He saw the impact of that statement wash over them. He also felt his future for the next three decades change dramatically.

After the prosecution rested, Judge Merrick told Mr. Garr that he would have time to put forth the defense's case in the morning. Before Ned was returned to his cell, he asked for a five-minute conference with his attorney, which was granted. They were shuffled off into the law library, which sounded more impressive than the reality of the room.

Ned and Garr sat on opposite sides of the table. They were alone in the small, windowless room, although an armed guard did stand watch outside the only door.

"Give it to me straight," Ned said. "What are our chances?"

"The same as they have been ever since the trial started. Not good."

"Thank you for being honest with me. I saw the look on the jury's face when the blood testimony was given. It wasn't good."

"Can you give me a good reason as to why a blood type that rare just happened to be on your jeans?"

"I can, but you would never believe me."

"If you can't convince me of the truth when I am on your side, what chance do we have to convince twelve neutral strangers?"

"Good point. What else do we have to put forth in our defense?"

"I hate to say it, but not much. I have a few character witnesses lined up for you, and I'll do my best to create some doubt regarding the validity of their evidence in my closing statement, but that's about it. We just have to hope that the D.A. didn't do enough to prove his side of the case."

Ned sat up, strumming his fingers for a long minute. "I know what I want to do. I want to get on the stand and tell the truth."

"Will that truth involve a confession for killing Mary Malone?"

"No. I told you that I didn't kill Mary Malone."

"That will open you up to cross-examination by Mr. King."

"Once they hear my story, I don't think that will matter."

"Alright, so how would you like me to question you? What should I ask?"

"Just ask me what happened on that night. I'll take it from there."

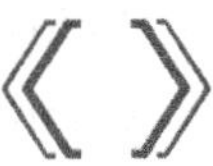

THE NEXT MORNING, THE jury shuffled in, ready to see if there would be any more surprise testimonies. They would not be disappointed. Judge Merrick entered the courtroom at nine o'clock sharp, greeted the jury, and told Mr. Garr to call his first witness.

Garr stood, looking even younger than normal with the spotlight fully fixed on him. He cleared his throat and then he said, "I'd like to call Ned Summers to testify."

Ned, who was wearing an inexpensive suit his father had bought for him, sprang up and walked to the witness box. He raised his right hand and swore to tell the truth, the whole truth, and nothing but the truth. He even added, "And I really will," at the end of it.

On his side of the courtroom, District Attorney King laid out a notebook and sat hunched over it, staring at Ned like a hawk stares down a scurrying mouse trying to cross an open space.

Garr stood well back from Ned and said, "Mr. Summers, please tell me what happened on the night of the murder."

"I will, sir," Ned began. "Although I might have to take you back a little earlier to make sense of all of it." Ned looked at Garr, who resignedly nodded at him.

"You see, that was not the first time I had lived through that night."

Silence filled the courtroom as everyone tried to parse exactly what he meant by that.

"I wish I could explain it better, but I lived through that night—went out with Mary, went out for a shake, then took her home—a lifetime before. The same thing happened. Mary disappeared that night, and then her body was found in Whitaker Park two days later. I didn't get arrested in that life because my dad came and took me out of the Chief's office before he got a chance to get a confession."

Ned locked eyes with his father, who seemed to have aged a dozen years in the previous month. The pain in William's eyes made Ned look away.

"I lived my whole life, and then I died, only to wake up right back here again. It was as if nothing had changed, but I still had all my memories of this previous life."

"Objection, your honor!" King shouted, jumping to his feet like he'd received an electrical prod in the posterior.

Judge Merrick, who had been completely in charge of the proceedings from the first moment on, looked flustered by the testimony.

King jumped into the silence. "Your honor, the defense is just trying to set up an appeal on an insanity plea. If this was going to be the defendant's testimony, we should have known in time to get him checked out by qualified psychiatric personnel."

Merrick looked at Garr, who said, "This testimony is a surprise to me, too, your honor."

The judge thought about his decision for several long seconds while every eye in the courtroom rested on him. "I believe in letting a defendant speak for themselves, whenever they choose to do so."

King opened his mouth to object, but Merrick held a hand up, silencing him.

Merrick looked down at Ned in the witness chair. "But I am not inclined to let you go too far afield, son. I won't have you make a mockery of my courtroom."

"I understand, Judge. I'll just tell the truth."

"Within limits, then, you may continue."

Ned gathered his thoughts and said, "I just wanted to explain, once and for all, what I was doing there in Whitaker Park that night. That's how I got the blood on my pants—I kneeled down next to Mary when Chief Deakins dropped her body there."

King again jumped to his feet with an objection. A murmur of conversation ran through the benches at the back of the room and even the jury exchanged glances with each other. Everyone's focus was on the judge, who was banging his gavel.

Everyone's except Ned's, that was. He was staring straight at Chief Deakins, who met Ned's gaze with narrowed eyes. There was an acknowledged truth between the two of them, but that was as far as that truth would go.

Judge Merrick restored order to the courtroom and then he turned to Ned. "Son, that is enough of that testimony. You can sit down."

"Thank you, sir. That's all I wanted to say."

Ned returned to his place beside Chad Garr and looked placidly ahead. The closing arguments were an anticlimax after Ned's testimony, but D.A. King did ask the jury to disregard his statement as grandstanding with an eye toward a future appeal.

Garr's argument came down to a preliminary plea for mercy for the mixed-up young man who sat before them. The jury was shown to the jury room to deliberate, but before an hour had passed, they were back in the courtroom—highly unusual for a murder trial.

The judge had given instructions to the jury as to what their potential findings could be: murder in the first degree, murder in the second degree, or innocent.

Fin Abergast, who had done everything he could to not be seated on the jury, had been elected the foreman. He stood tall and lean in his Levi's as he read the paper that he held out in front of him. He was born and bred in Polk County, but with the spotlight shining brightly on him, he affected a slight Texas twang to his mannerisms.

"We, the jury, in the case of Ned Daniel Summers, find the defendant—" He paused for a slight dramatic effect, and then picked up where he left off, saying, "Not guilty of first degree murder."

Chad Garr, who had been holding his breath, let it out in one elongated whoosh. Without thinking, he reached an arm over and laid it across Ned's shoulder.

That meant, at a minimum, that the death penalty was off the table.

Abergast continued, saying, "We the jury find the defendant guilty of murder in the second degree."

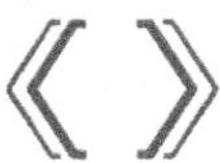

THE CROWD AT NED'S sentencing was much smaller than it had been at his trial. The townspeople guessed correctly when they said they had sucked the marrow out of the bone of this case.

Today, William Summers sat on one side of the courtroom, and Mr. and Mrs. Malone sat on the other, looking daggers at either William or Ned if they happened to glance their way. Victim statements had not yet come into vogue in the summer of 1952, so Judge Merrick simply announced the sentence: thirty-five years.

That sentence was at the high end of the sentencing range, but Judge Merrick had come to believe that Ned's testimony in his court had been exactly what D.A. King had said it was—an attempt to set up a future appeal on the grounds of Ned's forged incompetence to stand trial. Trial judges are used to having their work held under a microscope, but they don't like being played for a fool.

Chapter Thirty

Ned Summers sat on the bunk in his cell as he read a book. The Oregon State Penitentiary in Salem, Oregon, was going to be his new home for quite a while now. In all his years living at the cabin, he had never been much of a reader. There had always been too many things to attract his attention outside—too many projects and too many things to see.

With his world reduced primarily to this six-by-eight-foot cell, reading became his escape into the world at large. He volunteered to work in the prison library because he found that he read faster than he could get books brought to his cell.

He had started with Jack London books, but then a bookstore went out of business and donated boxes of used books to the prison. Inside one box, he found nearly fifty different books by Zane Gray, which proved to be very popular with the inmates who read. Even better for Ned was a collection of books by an author named Jim Kjelgaard.

Kjelgaard wrote books about animals and the outdoors. Reading *Snow Dog, Haunt Fox,* or *Big Red* was as close as Ned could come to transporting himself back to the cabin in the woods he missed so much. He knew he would never see his cabin again in this lifetime.

When Ned had decided to testify truthfully at his trial, he already knew what the course of his life would be. He knew he would be found guilty and sentenced to more years in prison than he would serve.

He didn't know for sure that if he died, he would wake up at some earlier point in his life, but it was a chance he was willing to take. He had figured that the worst case scenario meant that he would go on to whatever fate should have awaited him at the end of his first life. In the best case, he might get a third chance at the life he had messed up so badly. But the plans Ned devised in his mind were put asunder by his father.

As soon as Ned had been sentenced to thirty-five years in prison, William had sold the house in Middle Falls and moved into a rental in Salem. He got a job through the local union there and essentially built his life around visiting Ned at every opportunity.

During their first conversation after the trial, William had asked Ned, "Why? Why would you tell such a cockamamie story?"

Without blinking, Ned said, "Because it's the truth, Dad. The truth has to be worth something, doesn't it?"

They both knew there was nothing else to be said down that conversational path, and they never mentioned it again.

But the fact that William changed his whole life to be near the prison left Ned in a quandary. How could he stand to kill himself and leave his father behind when he had done so much for him?

He knew he couldn't, and so he resigned himself to doing a long stretch of time. He knew it wouldn't be thirty-five years, though, because he planned to carry out his original plan whenever his father died.

He went to prison in July of 1952, and he remembered that his father died in October of 1959. He knew he could do seven years. And, if his father happened to live longer in this lifetime, that was all to the good.

At present, it was a Sunday in September of 1957. It was another visitor's day. Ned knew his father would be there, simply because he had been there for every visitor's day since he had been incarcerated.

Ned put his book down and checked his reflection in the small metal mirror that hung next to his toilet. When he had lived in the wild, he had let his hair and beard grow long and crazy, but here in prison, he got a haircut every two weeks, and that kept his hair more in the current style.

He stood at the bars and waited for one of the guards to come take him to the visiting room. Even though he was in prison for murder, he didn't have to sit across from his visitors and talk on the phone like in the movies. There was a large room where families were allowed to gather and converse.

When Ned was let into the visiting room, he received a shock, as well as a reminder, that although things happened essentially the same way as when he first returned to Middle Falls, the farther away he got from those events, the more things changed.

William Summers sat at the same table he did every visiting day, but today, there was a woman with him. She looked a little younger than William, but not by much. She was a little heavy, but that may have just been because she was standing next to William, who was wiry-thin. His father shifted nervously from one foot to another.

Ned waved, then walked over and sat down opposite his father.

"Ned, this is Lucinda. Lucinda, Ned."

Ned held his hand out and shook Lucinda's hand.

"Pleased to meet you, Lucinda. This is a pretty big day. Dad's never brought anyone with him before. I don't know how much of a date it is to come to a penitentiary, though."

Lucinda blushed a little and smiled, which made her almost pretty. "I've been trying to get Will to bring me with him for months now, but he was nervous about it."

Lots of information in that sentence. She calls him Will. Never known anyone to call him Will before. And if she's been asking him for months, then you've been nervous about even telling me about her, Dad. We talk for hours, twice a month, but Lucinda never made it into the conversation.

"Well, I'm glad he finally brought you, although spending a few hours here isn't all that much of a treat." He caught his father's eye and smiled. "It's nice to have someone new to tell our stories to. This'll give us a whole new audience."

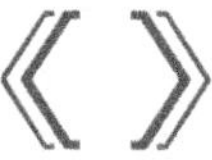

SIX MONTHS LATER, WILLIAM and Lucinda were married. They tried to arrange to have the ceremony held in the visitor's room, so Ned could attend, but the logistics of getting everyone else in proved to be too much.

Instead, the next time they visited, they brought in Kodak pictures. William looked stiff and uncomfortable in a new suit. Lucinda was flanked by her three daughters who served as bridesmaids. Ned noticed that no one stood with his father.

Ned shrugged and said, "That was where you belonged. I couldn't stand to put anyone else there."

William had been afraid that Ned would see the marriage as a betrayal of his mother, but that was ridiculous. Lucinda was warm and sweet and she made William happy. That had been all Ned had cared about since the trial.

William continued to come to visit every visitor's day. Most times, Lucinda came with him. On one Sunday when she couldn't make it, Ned had a serious conversation with his father.

"Dad, there's something I need to talk with you about."

William nodded, but he didn't say anything.

"I'll bet you've still got that insurance policy, don't you?"

"Of course."

"And I'll bet I'm still the beneficiary on it, aren't I?

"Yes."

"That's not right, Dad. You've got a wife now. And where I am, a bunch of money in the bank doesn't do me any good. I want you to call that insurance company and change the beneficiary to Lucinda."

William's eyes grew watery. "You make it sound like you're never going to get out of this place. I can't stand the thought of that. As long as I've had the policy for you, I feel like I'm still taking care of you."

"I'm going to do my best, Dad. But in the meantime, if something should happen to you, I want that money—and whatever you've got left over from selling the house in Middle Falls—to go to Lucinda."

William nodded, but he said, "I'm not about to just drop dead, you know. I've still got a little life left in me."

"I know, Dad," William said, hauling out the checkerboard they played on most every Sunday. "If you died, who would I beat at checkers?"

They never spoke of it again, but two years later, William Summers died, just as he had in Ned's first life. Lucinda continued to come and visit in Will's place. Ned was relieved to find that his father had done as he had asked and taken care of Lucinda.

It was wonderful of Lucinda to come and visit him, and he had grown to love her, too. However, it wasn't enough to keep him from executing his plan.

The month after his father died, Ned hung himself in his jail cell.

Chapter Thirty-One

Ned Summers opened his eyes just in time to see Stanley Dill wind up for a roundhouse punch.

"Wow! It worked!" Ned explained, as he easily backed away from the blow.

Stanley looked at him crossly. "What are you talking about? I'm about to clean your clock, that's all."

Ned stood up straight, dropped his hands, and said, "Stanley, I don't want to fight with you. And you don't want to fight with me, either, because Mr. Temple is about to come and put the collar on both of us."

"Don't chicken out now, Summers. I've been waiting for this since second grade, and nothing's gonna stop the beating." He swung wildly again, but Ned ducked out of the way again. "Goddamn it, Summers, stand still and fight!"

From outside the ring of boys, an authoritative voice said, "What have we here? Unscheduled fisticuffs? If you boys want to have at each other, let's go get the gloves on." It was Mr. Temple, right on schedule.

Dill squinted at Ned and said, "How'd you know?"

Ned ignored Dill and said, "Nah, that's okay, Mr. Temple. We were just foolin' around."

Temple looked from Ned's smiling face to Dill's red, angry one. "Is that true? Whatever this was, is all settled?"

"Yep!" Ned spouted.

Stanley Dill stared at the ground.

"Mr. Dill?"

"Okay," he said, dragging the two syllables out.

Temple put a strong hand on each of the two boys' shoulders. "Listen, men. Graduation is just a week away. You don't want to risk messing that up and making me call your parents when you're so close to matriculating from our fine institution, do you?"

"No," both Ned and Stanley agreed.

"Good!" Temple said, clapping both boys on the back. "But as long as I've got all of you here, I do have some extra credit work I could find for you..."

The crowd evaporated until it was just Ned and Mr. Temple standing alone.

Ned reached a hand out to Mr. Temple, who reflexively took it.

"Sorry, Mr. Temple. This was my fault. Won't happen again." Ned looked up at the wispy clouds in the blue late-spring day. He took a deep breath of the sweet air. "Isn't it a beautiful day?"

"It is," Temple agreed, before looking more closely at Ned. "Young Mr. Dill didn't hit you on the head before I got here, did he? Give your brains a little scramble?"

"No sir, I am one hundred percent good. It's amazing what a little change in your perspective can do for you."

Ned didn't wait for a response, but rather, he turned and jogged to the bicycle rack, grabbed his bike, and pedaled home. As he pedaled, he hummed a Buddy Holly song that wouldn't be written or recorded for another six years.

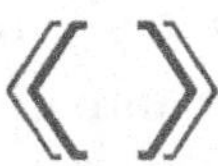

AT HOME, HE BUSTLED around, making dinner for him and William, who he knew would be home shortly.

He fried some bacon in a heavy cast iron frying pan to get some grease to fry the potatoes, while he molded some hamburger into patties.

I wonder if I get an endless number of do-overs like this, or is there a limit? Like maybe, three strikes and you're out? If so, I'd better get things right this time.

He sliced an onion and added it to the bacon grease before he dropped the sliced potatoes in. The smell of the bacon and onion cooking together rose from the pan and Ned inhaled deeply.

Those years in prison were tough. It was like everything in my life was gray. The walls were gray, the floors were gray, and my clothes were gray. All the life had been sucked out of my existence. I can never go back to a life like that, no matter what.

A few minutes later, William walked in, set his battered lunchbox on the countertop, and said, "Smells good."

He walked right by Ned to the bathroom to wash his hands. He didn't notice that Ned was grinning at him like an idiot.

When William emerged from the bathroom, Ned had already dished up the hamburger patties and had them waiting on the table.

William finally looked at Ned and noticed his smile. "You look happy today. What's going on with you?"

"Nothing special, Dad. I guess I'm excited for graduation next week. Trying to figure out what to do after that. Any ideas for me?"

"Getting a job is always a good first step."

Ned batted the glass Heinz Ketchup bottle with the palm of his hand, spreading ketchup over both his potatoes and the patty. He forked a big mouthful of potato into his mouth, and then tried talking around it.

"Is there anything you can do to help me with that?"

William set his fork down and stared at Ned. "I don't think I've ever seen you this hyped up. I guess you just woke up this morning and saw your whole life spreading out in front of you, didn't you?"

"That's pretty much exactly it, yep."

"Well, we do have an apprenticeship program down at the union hall. I don't know if you'd be interested in anything like that, but I'd be glad to stand for you."

"That would be great, Dad. Maybe I could keep working at the hardware store for a few months, and work in the apprentice program at the same time."

"You sure could. As soon as we get through graduation, I'll bring you up for the program."

Ned used his butter knife to scrape the remaining bits of food together, then loaded it on his fork.

"I think that's the fastest I've ever seen you eat."

"It just seemed extra good tonight. Really hit the spot."

William looked down at his own plate, which was still mostly full.

"I don't think I've ever told you, Dad, but I appreciate everything you've ever done for me."

William waved the remark away, wordlessly.

"I mean it. No matter what's happened to me, you've always been the one thing in my life I could count on."

"Your mother would have done the same, if she had been able to be here."

That's right, isn't it? For you, Mom just died a few years ago. For me, she's been dead more than sixty years.

"Well, I've got a little homework to finish up," Ned said, carrying his plate to the kitchen.

"Still piling it on you, right up to the bitter end, huh?"

"It's okay. After this week, I should never have to write another English essay."

"You go on then. Since you cooked, I'll clear the table and wash the dishes."

Ned walked back to his bedroom and closed the door. He sat on the edge of his bed and looked around at his familiar room.

So many decisions to make. I thought I had everything figured out when I was sitting in my cell, but somehow being here, everything feels different. I've got some big decisions to make, and not a lot of time to make them.

Chapter Thirty-Two

The next morning, Ned got up, feeling the same groggy, disoriented feeling he had the last time he had made the time jump.

Something about doing that wears me out. Or maybe it just takes a little while for all of me to catch up. Wish I knew a little more about what was happening with all this.

Ned woke up that morning more confident in his decisions than he had been the night before.

He had decided to go to school, not just today, but up until he was released for graduation. His last life had felt disjointed right from the time he had woken up back in 1952, and he blamed a lot of that on the fact that he blew off school.

So, despite the fact that he didn't really remember what his classes were, or what his locker was, or the names of a lot of people he was going to run into, he was going to school.

At 7:45, he hopped on his bike. Halfway to school, he heard, "Yo, Summers!"

Ned turned toward the voice. "Hey, Stink, how's it going."

Stink shrugged. "It's Friday, so I don't have to go to school tomorrow. So, good, I guess."

Ned looked at Stink. He wasn't tall, or good looking. He wasn't a good athlete or a particularly great student. In fact, if they weren't friends, Ned likely wouldn't have ever noticed him.

"Hey, Stink?"

"Yeah?"

"Does it bother you that everyone calls you that?"

"What? Stink? No, it's my name."

"Not really, it's not. Would you rather be called something else?"

"Yeah," Stink said. "I dream about everyone calling me Vernon. What's with you today anyway? You just jealous cuz you don't have a cool nickname like I do?"

Ned leaned back on his bike, taking his hands off his handlebars. It had been a long time since he had really ridden a bike, but he was pleased to find that he kept his balance with only a little wobble.

"Yep, you figured me out. Just a little jealous."

Stink took two quick steps to his right and nudged the back tire of the bike, which nearly sent Ned sprawling over the handlebars.

"Jesus, Stink!"

Stink ignored the near-catastrophe that he caused. "So whatcha got going tonight? Nothing at all, like usual?"

Great question. I guess I've got a date with the prettiest girl in town. I didn't ask Dad if I could borrow the car last night, though, because I'm not planning on going. I've been on that date two times and it didn't help me at all.

"Nothin'. I've got nothin' going."

"Another boring weekend in Middle Falls, then," Stink said.

I don't know if I'd go that far. Hopefully, I can stop a murder.

NED MANAGED TO SURVIVE his first day as an eighty-some year old man attending high school. He found that as a senior, just a week from graduating, not a lot was expected of him. He did his best to remember or figure out which class he had at which time. Once he managed that, he sat in the back, appeared to pay attention and did his best not to draw attention to himself.

In sixth period English, Stanley Dill and a few of his friends were obviously talking about and making fun of him, trying to get a rise, but Ned ignored them. If you live long enough, you figure out that petty annoyances come mostly from petty people, and so were nothing to be concerned about.

As soon as the final bell rang, Ned jumped on his bike and rode to Smith & Sons grocery. He dropped the bike on the front sidewalk, went in and stood in line at Mary Malone's register.

She didn't recognize him until he got to the front of the line, but when she did, Ned could see she was surprised to see him there.

"Oh! Didn't expect to see you for a few hours."

"That's why I came by. I want to let you know that I can't take you out tonight."

A cloud passed over Mary's pretty face. "Oh? I was really looking forward to seeing the movie."

But not necessarily thrilled about seeing me, I'd bet.

"Sorry, Mary. My dad needs me to help him tonight, and I can't tell him no."

Mary didn't reply immediately. There was a woman in line behind Ned, ready to be checked out, but Mary didn't seem to care too much. It was obvious that she didn't really like Ned's reason for canceling their date. Finally, she simply shrugged and said, "Oh well."

Ned stepped aside and Mary began to ring up the woman's groceries. She had apparently forgotten Ned, as she didn't say anything more to him.

Ned eased out onto the sidewalk, one more thing checked off his to-do list.

He had a nice ride home and even took a loop around the service road at Whitaker Park.

Last life, I thought this was the spot where everything happened, but it was just a convenient dumping ground for Chief Deakins. Why would he choose here? With his prowler, he could have driven her out on Forest Ser-

vice Road and carried her a few yards back into the woods and she might never have been found. Why here?

There were no answers to be found, so he headed home and cooked a dinner of pork chops and corn on the cob.

Over dinner, William observed, "You seem a lot quieter tonight than you were last night."

It took Ned some time to answer. *How can I explain all this, Dad? I tried telling the absolute truth last life, and that didn't turn out good at all.*

"It's nothing, really. Just kind of a girl problem."

"I don't know that I'm the best person to advise you about that. Women are mysterious creatures that I have never come close to understanding."

"Nothing to worry about, I'll figure it out."

Thirty minutes later, they had finished dinner and done the dishes.

William had stopped at the store and picked up the replacement tube they needed for the radio. When Ned came out of the kitchen after doing the dishes, the radio was lit up and William was tuning it in.

"Hey, Dragnet's coming on soon. Want to listen?"

"You bet, Dad."

The rest of the evening passed easily. After *Dragnet* and *Arthur Godfrey's Talent Scouts*, Ned looked through the hall closet until he found their old checkerboard.

"How about it, Dad? Feel like getting whooped in a game or two before bed?"

"When did you get so cocky?" William asked, putting *The Middle Falls Chronicle* aside.

Ned took the first two games, but he threw the third game, just as he had done so often at the penitentiary.

"I think I'll quit on a winning streak of one," William said. "It's getting late."

Ned glanced at the clock. It was already nine.

"Goodnight, Dad. See you in the morning."

Ned went to his room and closed the door, but didn't get undressed.

He waited until William was done in the bathroom and gone to bed. He gave him half an hour to fall asleep, then, sock-footed, slipped through the house to the back door.

He grabbed both the .22, the flashlight and his jacket, then quietly opened the back door. He slipped out into the cooling night air.

Chapter Thirty-Three

Ned had spent years sitting in prison, thinking about the events that were about to unfold. Thinking of the timing of things, the order things must have happened in. Even with all that time to think and plan, he felt under-prepared. He was so limited in the tools at his disposal, and he had so little time to get things in order each time he woke up back in 1952.

He wanted to believe that simply not going out on the date with Mary would be enough, but when he was honest with himself, he couldn't believe that. Mary's death had been already in motion when she agreed to go out with Ned. He didn't have anything to do with it, and so taking himself out of the equation wouldn't change much.

Ned zipped up his light jacket and walked his bike down to the street so he wouldn't accidentally wake William by crunching the tires over gravel.

It was a few minutes after ten. If he had gone on his date with Mary, he would have just dropped her off. Because he hadn't been able to ascertain what time she snuck out last time, he still suffered from a shortage of information. The only thing he knew for sure was that sometime after midnight, Chief Deakins would pull his car into Whitaker Park and dump Mary's body.

What happened between this time and that time was still a mystery.

But I know who the key to that mystery is. Chief Deakins.

That afternoon, Ned had found the address of the Deakins' home in the Middle Falls phone book. Now, he rode through the shadows to that address. He needed to find where Deakins was and stick with him.

That was the real challenge of course. Ned had two choices for transportation—his bicycle or his dad's truck. The bike was perfect for stealth, but it made it tough to keep up with a moving car. He had eliminated his dad's Dodge, as it was too noticeable and noisy, as evidenced by the woman's testimony at his trial.

Chief Deakins didn't live too far away from Ned's house, but then, nothing was more than a mile or two away in Middle Falls. Most of the houses had porch lights on, which made it easy for Ned to identify which house was Deakins'.

Ten minutes later, Ned found the correct house, but his heart dropped. There were lights on inside and he could see a woman walking around the living room, almost like she was pacing, but there was no squad car and no sign of the chief.

Ned pushed on back toward downtown. At Coleman's Furniture, he took a left and pulled up to the police station. It was dark and buttoned up tight. He found a spot half a block down under a tree where he thought he would look inconspicuous and watched the station, hoping that the chief would come by there for something.

What do I do if I can't find you tonight? An innocent girl will be killed, but this time there will be no trail back to me. I'll finally be able to live my life however I want. I can work with dad, or I can go out and live in the cabin again.

Even as the thought rolled through his mind, Ned was shaking his head. There was truth in the statement, but it also seemed like a coward's way out.

I'll do whatever I can, which is always the best that I can. If that doesn't work, I'll have a clear conscience.

He stood in the deep shadows for another twenty minutes, but he grew increasingly anxious.

I could be standing here, and he could be murdering her right now.

At that moment, a memory rose unbidden in his mind.

Ned saw himself behind the wheel of his father's truck. He had been driving toward Whitaker Park. As he turned right, Chief Deakins turned left right in front of him. Deakins looked up into the truck and saw Ned. Ned looked down into the prowler and saw Deakins.

That was the night of the murder. Deakins was out patrolling the streets. He's not at home, or here, he's driving around town. Now, where was I when I passed him, and what time was that?

Neither of those answers sprang easily to Ned's mind, so he got back on his bike and pedaled in the general direction of Whitaker Park.

That's the direction I was heading when I ran into him. Maybe I can do it again.

Ned spent the next thirty minutes crisscrossing the streets around Whitaker Park on his bicycle.

He felt the passage of time with increasing urgency, sure that the more time passed, the less likely he would be to stop the murder.

He was breathing hard and sweat was pouring down his face as he saw the first set of headlights he had seen in a long time.

He veered his bike off onto a sidewalk and behind a parked car. He straddled his bike and found himself holding his breath, when he saw the familiar rooftop lights of a Middle Falls squad car. It passed him doing a sedate twenty miles an hour in the direction from which he had just come.

Ned lifted his bike, turned it around, and began pumping steadily after the car. Even as slow as it was going, Ned had to put his all into keeping up with Deakins.

Chief Deakins meandered through the quiet streets of Middle Falls. If he had a pattern or destination, it wasn't immediately noticeable to Ned.

Ned was focused on one thing—the growing pain in his legs as he did his best to stay within sight.

Deakins finally turned left on the main drag and headed east.

Ned was just close enough to see his taillights and turn signal indicate a left turn. By the time he had caught up to that spot, the police car was gone out of sight.

Chapter Thirty-Four

Ned felt like he was about to hyperventilate after trying so hard to keep up with the police car.

He dismounted and leaned over, trying to catch his breath. There was no sign of the car anywhere ahead. Disgusted with himself for losing sight of it, Ned hunkered down and let himself rest for a few moments. Finally, his breathing returned to normal and he started pedaling along Middle Falls' main drag.

Each time he came to a cross street, he slowed and looked both ways, searching for any sign of Deakins. Just as he was about to give up hope, he rode up to Marv's Diner. Marv's was famous in Middle Falls for opening early and staying open late. After ten at night, there were only two places you could get something to eat—your own kitchen, or Marv's.

The Middle Falls squad car was parked right in front of Marv's.

I think I learned my lesson. I can't keep up with him, no matter how slow he's driving. I need a new plan.

Ned rode past the diner and looked inside. It was the only light shining on the entire street. Inside, Ned could see an old woman standing behind a cash register, talking to Chief Deakins, who had a cup of coffee and a piece of pie in front of him.

Ned jumped off his bike and ran it alongside the building. He ditched the bike in the shadows and crept back along until he could peek around the corner. Deakins had finished his pie and had stood up. He hitched up his gun belt and walked toward the register.

Now or never.

Hunkering over, Ned hustled over to the cop car, reached the back door and tried to open it.

It was locked.

Of course.

He slid up to the front of the car, lifting his head just enough that he could peer over the hood and see inside Marvin's. Deakins was still standing, chatting up the old lady behind the register.

Ned tried the driver's door. Miraculously, it opened. Unfortunately, the dome light also came on, which made Ned feel exceptionally exposed.

Ned snaked his arm inside the front seat, reached around and unlocked the back door. The car was relatively new—a 1950 Ford—but even so, police car technology wasn't advanced yet. There was no steel mesh or polyglass between the front seat and the back. This car was never intended to arrest and transport dangerous fugitives.

As soon as he had the back door unlocked, Ned shut the front door with a click, then leaned into it to shut it the rest of the way. He was just about to climb into the back seat when he heard the door to Marv's open with a 'Ding!'

Ned had his hand on the back door handle, but he froze.

A moment later, he heard the woman's voice from inside Marv's say, "Chief, you forgot something." The door to the restaurant slid shut.

Ned didn't hesitate. He threw open the back door, leaped inside, reached around behind him, and pulled the door shut.

The backseat of the Ford was spacious, but it was a rear-wheel drive, so there was a hump in the middle of the floor. There was just enough room for Ned to lay flat on the floor between the backseat and the front. The hump where the drive shaft ran was right between Ned's belly and his groin.

Not the most comfortable position in the world, but I'm in. Wherever he goes, I'll go. Whatever he sees, I'll see. I'll finally know what happens to Mary.

A few seconds later, the driver's door opened and the dome light illuminated once again. Ned held his breath. He was sure that the next thing he would hear would be, "Hey! What the hell? What are you doing back there?"

Instead, he heard the car door slam, Deakins turn the key and the engine roar to life. When the chief leaned back in his seat, Ned could feel the pressure on his back and butt. Again, he was afraid that would give him away.

Instead, Deakins let out a belch, followed by a "Well, excuse the hell right out of me," said to no one in particular.

Deakins put the car in reverse and backed out onto the main drag.

Ned closed his eyes and tried to tell which way he was going each step of the way, but soon realized he was lost.

Deakins turned left, right, then left again before he slowed down and seemed to pull over.

Ned heard him reach across the seat with a groan and unlock the passenger door.

They sat like that for several minutes, engine idling, not moving.

Finally, Ned heard the passenger door open.

"Hey, sweet girl," Deakins said. "I thought maybe you weren't going to make it tonight."

"No, I just had a little trouble getting out of the house. Mom had an idea something was up, so she was playing bloodhound on me like she does sometimes."

Definitely Mary's voice.

"C'mon, let's go out to our spot."

Ned twisted onto his left side as quietly as possible, so he could see out the back window of the car. At first, he saw street lights flit across the window, then felt the bump of the wheels going over the railroad tracks, then felt nothing but smooth pavement. The only light out the back window was from the stars.

They drove on the main highway out of town for a few miles, then turned south. With a sudden certainly, Ned knew that they had turned down Forest Service Road where his cabin was. He had a sudden, freakish intuition that they might be heading out to use the cabin as some kind of a love getaway, but quickly put the idea out of his head.

They drove down the bumpy dirt road and gravel road for several miles, then turned left on another spur road that Ned had never gone down.

Deakins and Mary hadn't spoken the whole way.

Finally, Deakins pulled the car to a stop but didn't turn the engine off.

Again, Ned held his breath, fearful that even the sound of his breathing would give him away.

Chapter Thirty-Five

Ned heard the creaking of the front seat as Deakins leaned across toward Mary.

"Stop it, Michael."

"Honey, we get so little time together. I just want to make the most of it."

"You're in a hurry to have sex, you mean."

"Aren't you?"

Again, a shuffling sound came from the front of the car.

Ned heard an exasperated "hunh" from Mary, and then Deakins moved back to his side of the car.

"What's the matter with you tonight?"

"I've been telling you for weeks—months, really—but you just aren't listening to me. I don't want to do this anymore."

"What, come to the cabin? We can't go to the motel in town—it wouldn't take ten minutes for word to get around."

"I mean, it's not just the cabin. It's not the difference between a cabin and motel. It's *us.* I don't want to do *us* anymore."

"Why?"

"You know why. I'm just not going to do this sneaking around anymore. When we first started, you told me that you and your wife were getting a divorce. You told me you were mostly separated already, that you and she never slept together, and that the divorce would be final within the year. And that was *two* years ago. Do you know what's changed since then? Absolutely nothing."

"I know, I know. You're right. Sometimes these things take time."

"I saw your wife in the grocery store last week."

"You didn't say anything, did you?"

"You know I didn't. If I had, she'd have probably met you at home with a frying pan in her hand. But I did notice something when she was in the store."

Mary paused, but Deakins didn't jump in to say anything.

"Your wife is very pretty, Michael, and she takes care of herself. She's always dressed nicely. But when I saw her in the store last week, her dress couldn't cover up her tummy, which looked very damned pregnant to me."

Ned, laying deathly still in the backseat, marveled at the fact that there was so much more to the story than what he had known, even after living two other lifetimes.

"So, is that right? Is she pregnant?"

"Yes, but—"

"There's nothing I need to hear from you after that 'yes, but,' thank you very much. That tells me everything I need to know."

Mary threw the car door open and hurried out. She didn't slam the door behind her and Ned could hear the sound of her crying.

With a muttered curse, Deakins opened his door and got out as well.

Ned lay across the back, unsure of what to do.

Is this the moment he kills her? I've got to look and try to stop it.

Ned lifted his head until he could see above the passenger seat. He could see that not only was the engine running, but Deakins hadn't turned the headlights off. Mary stood off to the right of the car, sobbing. Deakins stood in front of her, holding her shoulders and trying to explain.

Ned couldn't hear what he was saying, but after the conversation in the car, he didn't really need to. He eased the .22 pistol out of his jacket pocket and held it in his sweaty right hand.

If he makes a move to hurt her, I'll jump out and stop him. I won't let him kill her again.

Deakins pointed to the door of the cabin.

"Come on, just come inside and we can talk about it. We can figure this out. I won't lose you."

"You don't get it. You've already lost me."

Deakins turned away in frustration. As soon as his back was turned, Mary turned and ran down a path into the woods. Over her shoulder, she shouted, "Just go away! Leave me alone!"

"You're ten miles away from your house. I'm not going to leave you out here!" Deakins shouted after her. He stood, his hands on his hips, waiting for her to answer, but she didn't.

"God *damn* it," Deakins said, then turned and strode back toward the car.

Ned ducked down behind the back seat, afraid that he had been spotted.

Deakins jumped back inside the squad car and slammed the door behind him. He drummed his fingers loudly against the steering wheel.

"I oughta just leave you here and let you walk home." Deakins stepped on the accelerator and gunned the engine loudly. "In fact, you know what? Screw it, that's exactly what I'm going to do."

Deakins slammed the car into reverse and gunned it back down the spur road to Forest Service Road. He threw his arm over the front seat to look out the back window and his hand rested just a few inches above Ned's shoulder.

Deakins hit the main Forest Service road, dropped it into drive, and accelerated away. Ned could tell that they were going much faster on the way out than the way they had in.

Dumb ass. You've got a cabin out here, so you should know that there are deer everywhere. Going this fast, you could end up with one flying through your windshield.

Almost as if Deakins had heard Ned's thought, he sighed and slowed down. By the time he got to the highway, he had dropped to a normal speed. He sat at the T-intersection between the gravel road and the highway, idling the engine for a long minute. There was no other traffic in sight.

Finally, he pulled out onto the highway, backed up, and then turned back down the road he had just come.

"Come on," Deakins said to himself, "be a man. Do the right thing. God knows, I've done little enough of that the last few years." He was quiet the rest of the way back to the turnoff to his cabin.

He pulled up in front of the cabin, and got out of the vehicle, shutting the door behind him.

"Come on, Mary!" he shouted. "I'm sorry! Come on, I'll give you a ride home. You don't want to snag your clothes on the blackberry bushes."

Again, Ned lifted up and looked over the passenger seat.

Deakins stood at the front of the car, the headlights illuminating him from behind.

He cupped his hands around his mouth and shouted "Mary!" once more. Then he dropped his hands and ran forward to the edge of the woods.

He kneeled down beside something, but Ned had a tough time seeing around him.

Suddenly, Deakins stood and his face was twisted in a knot of pain. His right hand flew to his forehead.

When he stood, Ned could see what he had kneeled beside.

It was the body of Mary Malone.

Chapter Thirty-Six

Ned's heart sank.

A million thoughts raced through his mind.

Three lives, and I still can't save a girl I know is going to be murdered. And, *It wasn't Deakins after all.* And, *Then who in the hell was it?* And finally, *Oh my God, he's going to put her in the trunk. Will he see me?*

While Ned's mind was racing, it was apparent that Deakins' mind had turned off. He first knelt, and then sat, in the dirt beside the body. This war veteran, who had undoubtedly seen many bodies destroyed by bullets, had never seen a beautiful young girl's body crumpled and lifeless like this.

For long minutes, both Deakins and Ned held their particular positions, unmoving. Deakins broke the stalemate by finally standing up, and dusting off the dirt and pine needles first from his knees, then his backside. He took a deep breath and walked back to the car. He turned the engine off and pulled the keys out.

Ned did his level best to melt down into the floorboards of the backseat.

I have no idea what he would do if he found me out here now, but I don't think any of it would be good.

Deakins walked around to the back of the squad car, but he was blind to everything and did not see Ned. He opened the trunk and removed a roll of Visqueen that had been stashed there.

When Ned heard Deakin's boots crunch past the car, he once again pushed up and looked over the seat. He watched Deakins drop the roll of plastic onto the ground while he held onto one end of it. He was facing Mary's body and had his back to Ned.

Here's my chance.

Ned sat up and felt a spasm in his back from lying in the hunched position for so long. He ignored it and reached behind him, opening the back driver's side door as quietly as humanly possible. He slid out, feet first, until he was kneeling on the ground beside the car.

He stopped, waited, and listened. The normal night sounds of the forest, which were still a familiar soundtrack to Ned, even after so many years away, were absent. The birds, bugs, and animals were silent, waiting for man to depart.

Ned swung the door closed and pushed on it until it latched quietly. He stood part way up and peered through the window and windshield at Deakins. He had rolled the plastic out and moved Mary's body onto it.

Keeping the squad car between him and Deakins, Ned backed away until he found the cover of the edge of the forest. He was just about to melt into the trees and be safe when his heels ran into a small, fallen tree. He lost his balance and, although he pinwheeled his arms for balance, he fell over backward. He crashed into the underbrush with a sound that reverberated into the quiet night.

Deakins jumped to his feet, ran back to the squad car, and retrieved his flashlight. He took a dozen quick steps, holding the light in his left hand and his service revolver in his right.

Shit. He knows there's a murderer around, and I end up thrashing around like a gut-shot buck.

Deakins wasn't sure where the noise had come from and he ended up searching an area twenty-five feet from where Ned had fallen. He crashed around through the underbrush, arcing the flashlight's beam this way and that for what felt like hours. Eventually, he gave up and went back to the grisly business of wrapping up Mary's body and putting it in the trunk.

Once he had accomplished that, he walked around the side of the car. Before he got in, he looked down at the rear door on the driver's side. It was latched closed, but there was a small gap that showed it wasn't shut tight.

Deakins put his hip into the door, shutting it completely. He pulled the flashlight out and crisscrossed it around the entire area.

Ned put his face in the dirt and lay completely still.

Eventually, Deakins tossed the flashlight onto the front seat, then climbed in and backed the car down the spur until he hit Forest Service Road.

Ned continued to lie still until long after the sound of the Ford's engine had faded into the night.

Finally, he stood up, swiped at a few of the places where the blackberry bushes had nipped at him, and walked to where he had seen Mary's body. He got his flashlight out and shined it on the grass where Deakins had placed the plastic-encased body. The grass was flattened, but it was already springing back up. Ned kneeled down and peered closer, aided by the white light of the flashlight. There were small drops of blood just about everywhere.

It's not so much to where the next good rain won't wash it all away. A few days from now, there will probably be no evidence a murder was ever committed here.

He moved the beam of light around, looking to see if he could find bullet casings. If there had ever been any, Deakins had picked them up and carried them away.

I am so baffled. If Deakins didn't murder her—and I know he didn't now—then who else would? Who would have a motive? I can't believe it was just some random guy walking through the deep woods with a .22 and happened upon her in the fifteen minutes we were gone. I've lived in these woods too long to believe that.

He shined the flashlight on his watch. It was just after midnight. Deakins' words rang in his ears. *It's ten miles to home!* Ned slipped the flashlight back into one pocket, then set out for home.

He didn't notice the dark form in the cabin's window, watching him.

Chapter Thirty-Seven

Ned woke up at eight-thirty the next morning. He hadn't gotten back home until after three the night before, and he was still tired and a little sore.

He glanced at the clock beside his bedside table, and then he rolled over, punched his pillow, and closed his eyes, ready for a few more hours of sleep. Before he could drift off, he replayed the events of the night before.

I didn't save Mary again. But what does that mean? It means an innocent girl died for no reason. It also means I know where the murder took place now. Of course, I thought I knew that during my last lifetime, too.

Ned tossed around and stared at the wall.

But what does it all mean to me? Three times I've lived, and three times Mary's been killed. Maybe I can't stop that. Maybe I'm not supposed *to stop that in some big, cosmic way. At least in this life, I shouldn't be under a microscope. I wasn't the last person to see her alive. I didn't haunt the neighborhood around her house or kneel in her blood at the park this time. I should be able to live whatever life I want to, right? Get a job and—*

Ned sat up straight in bed.

Shit! A job! I've got to be at Coppens' in half an hour!

Ned flew out of bed, got dressed, grabbed a few handfuls of cereal, tossed them down his throat, and went to jump on his bike—which wasn't there.

I'm losing my mind. Of course it's not there. I left it in the grass next to Marv's last night. I am such an idiot.

He ran back into the house, looked up the number for Coppens' Hardware, and dialed the number.

Mrs. Coppens seemed to be very surprised to hear from her yard boy, who should be coming into work at any second.

"Ned? Is that you? Why aren't you here?"

"That's why I'm calling, Mrs. Coppen. My alarm didn't go off. I'm leaving the house now, but I don't have my bike, so I'm going to be a little late."

"We're going to have to dock you for this."

"Of course. Of course. I'm leaving my house now and I will run. I'll be there in twenty minutes."

Mrs. Coppen hung up without saying anything more.

Ned put on his tennis shoes and set out for the hardware store at a run.

He survived the withering glances from the Coppens and managed to get his work done. As he left the hardware store, he was acutely aware of where he was and what he was doing. He casually walked the three blocks from the hardware store to Marv's Café.

He kept his hands in his pockets and did everything but whistle innocently as he passed by and cut down the side of the building.

His bicycle was right where he had left it.

One advantage of having an old, piece of crap bike is that no one wants to steal it.

He rode down Main Street toward home.

It's Saturday. Mary's body won't be discovered until sometime late Sunday or early Monday. Between now and then, I've just got to stay away from Whitaker Park. Probably the best thing to do is stay home and wait for the storm to pass.

That's exactly what he did.

He and William had dinner like always on Saturday night, then listened to the radio for an hour or so before turning in.

The next day, Ned washed his dad's car, then started their old mower. He was mowing the dirt patch that they called a front yard.

Chief Deakins pulled to the curb in front of their house before Ned was halfway finished.

I'll say this for you, Chief. You're consistent.

Ned waved innocently, as though he hadn't already had essentially this conversation twice already.

Deakins got out of his prowler and opened the gate of the white picket fence. He looked at the patchy front yard and smiled at Ned. "Gotta keep those weeds under control, don't you?"

Ned squinted into the afternoon sun.

How can you be so goddamned cold-blooded? Two nights ago, you were trying to cheat on your wife with a girl ten years younger than you. Then you found her dead body and you dumped it. Now here you are, calm and collected, pretending like you're my friend. You're a piece of work.

"Are you Ned Summers?"

"Yes, sir."

"I'm just doing a little look into a missing person case. I'm sure it's nothing, but I have to follow up. Did you have a date with Mary Malone this last Friday night?"

"No, sir. I was supposed to, but my dad needed me to help him with some things after work that day, so I had to cancel. I stopped by the grocery store that afternoon and told her."

"Shame to cancel a date with such a pretty girl, isn't it?"

"Yes, sir, it was. Not as bad as getting my butt kicked up between my shoulder blades by my dad, though."

Deakins laughed. "I see you've got a dad just like mine." He lowered his voice and leaned forward. "Just between you and me, we're both better off for it."

"Yessir."

"How well did you know Mary?"

"Hardly at all. I just saw her in the grocery store, thought she was pretty, and asked her out. She said yes." Ned said this last with a shrug, as if he still couldn't quite believe that, either.

Deakins looked at Ned's stocky frame, all five-feet-eight-inches of it, and studied his completely forgettable face, dirty jeans, and T-shirt. It was obviously a mystery to him as well.

"Did you say Mary was missing?"

"Yeah, but I'm sure it's nothing. I think it's probably just a misunderstanding of some sort or another."

Sure you do, you lying sack of shit.

"Well, I'll let you get back to mowing your dirt," Deakins said with a smirk.

When he turned his back to go through the gate, Ned couldn't help himself. He gave him the quick one-finger salute.

Chapter Thirty-Eight

Ned Summers may have led three lives, but none of them were even remotely similar. His first life, he spent more than fifty years happily banished to the cabin in the woods. He spent almost all of his second in prison. That meant that even though he was on his third pass through the same time period, so much of it was new to him.

He never became a suspect in the murder of Mary Malone. In fact, no arrests were ever made in the case. As much as he had wanted to stop the murder from happening, once he failed at that, he did his best to put it behind him and focus on living his life.

He graduated with his class, and then William helped him get into the apprentice program in the local union hall. While most of his friends were either going to college or working entry-level jobs for seventy-five cents an hour, Ned learned how to operate heavy equipment and made three times the pay of his peers.

He was the first from his group of friends to be able to buy a nice truck of his own. Ned had enough money to move out on his own, but since he still remained what Stink had called him so long ago—the dateless wonder—he saw no reason to move out of his dad's place. He and William made the difficult transition from living together as parent and child to living as roommates. Ned paid his share of the expenses and they were both happy.

He couldn't say he loved his job, or that it really fulfilled him, but he didn't mind it. He liked being around his dad a lot because with each year that passed, he knew that was drawing to an end.

In early 1959, knowing that William's apparent expiration date was on the horizon, Ned convinced him to go in and get a full checkup.

William thought that was crazy. He was only in his early fifties and he felt great. Still, he did it for Ned. The results were exactly what William had expected—he was told he had no issues at all. Of course, in 1959, doctors still smoked while they examined their patients.

Ned accepted the fact that there were certain things that were inevitable in a lifetime and apparently his father's death was one of those things.

In early October, 1959, the inevitable arrived. William collapsed, although this time, Ned was there to catch him, having not left his side since the previous week. There was no need to call an ambulance because Ned got him to the hospital quicker himself, hoping that would make some difference.

In the end, the scene played out the way it had in his first life. William hung on for a few weeks, and he and Ned made plans to go out to the cabin in a few weeks. Ned became friends with the doctors and nurses and talked them into making an exception to their visiting hours. Ned only left his father's side when he needed to go home to shower and change his clothes.

In this life, he was with his father and held his hand as William closed his eyes and took his last breath.

Ned laid his head on the bed and cried.

It was hard watching his father die, of course, but it was also the third time he had been through it, and he knew that he had done everything he possibly could for him. He once again arranged for a funeral so William's friends could say goodbye.

This time, he had the presence of mind to ask the mystery woman he hadn't recognized at his father's first funeral who she was. She was dressed in black and wore a hat with a veil. When she lifted it to speak to Ned, she revealed an elegant, beautiful face.

"You must be William's son. I'm Nancy Sturgis. I knew your father when we were much younger." When she saw understanding register in Ned's face, she added, "Before he met your mother."

Ned hugged her and thanked her for coming.

For the next few decades, Ned enjoyed the technological marvels he had never taken part in during his earlier lives. He and his father had bought a television in 1957, but in 1965, he bought a Sylvania in-cabinet color television. It had a record player on one end, the television in the middle, and room for a bar on the other end.

He bought new appliances for the kitchen, all of which were matching avocado greens, but he grew to regret that choice through the rest of the seventies. By the early eighties, he replaced them all with solid white appliances. He liked those much better.

Ned also fixed up the cabin and spent his vacations and many of his weekends there. He wasn't a hermit like he was in his first life, but somehow, he had a hard time connecting with people. It felt like the fact that he was living his life over and over put a barrier between him and everyone else in the world.

About the time of his fiftieth birthday, in 1984, Mary Malone began to once again fill his thoughts. He took flowers to her grave each Memorial Day, as there was no one else to do it. Her parents had both passed away, and her little sister had moved to the Midwest long since.

Ned Summers didn't have the most scintillating, amazing life, but he knew that at least he'd had a life this time around. Mary had never gotten that chance. The more he thought about it, the more he realized he had all the information he needed to stop her murder. He'd known that since 1952, of course, but he'd done his best to put that thought out of his mind. After the unfulfilling lives he had lived, he chose to be selfish.

Now, he felt just that—selfish—and didn't like the feeling.

One late May afternoon in 1984, Ned sat in what had once been his father's house, which was now his. A baseball game was on his newest television—a Curtis Mathes, without the record player or built-in bar—watching an Atlanta Braves game on TBS. Dale Murphy was at the plate for the Braves, but Ned wasn't really watching.

I know what will happen if I start over. I'll end up being punched by Stanley Dill in front of the high school, and I'll have a little over twenty-four hours to stop the murder.

He clicked the power button on the remote and the television clicked off.

I've put it off long enough. There's no one here that will particularly miss me. I'm going to do it.

Chapter Thirty-Nine

Ned Summers opened his eyes. He easily batted away the wild swing from Stanley Dill. The momentum nearly made Stanley fall down and Ned gave him an easy shove to put him the rest of the way down.

"Stanley, if that's the best you can do, you need to consider who you pick a fight with."

Dill pushed himself up on one knee, then bull-rushed Ned, which was exactly what Ned thought he would do. Ned took one quick step to the left, put his hip into Stanley, and used the taller boy's own momentum to flip him completely over. He landed on his back with an audible thud and all the breath pushed out of him.

Ned stood casually over him. "Tell me when you've had enough."

Dill wasn't ready to admit defeat, but as he lay on his back like a flipped-over turtle, gasping desperately to get some oxygen back into his system, he didn't look like much of a threat.

Ned sensed a disruption behind him and turned to see Mr. Temple push his way through the ring of boys.

"That'll be enough," Temple said when he reached the inner circle. He took in Dill lying on his back in the grass and Ned standing beside him, not even breathing hard. Temple's instant schoolyard triage noticed there was no blood, no obviously broken bones, and no eyes swelled shut.

"Boys, it's a beautiful day. I don't care what you're fighting about," Temple said, "but I'm sure there's something better you can be doing."

The rest of the boys saw that any chance of fighting was over. They turned and slipped away before Temple could even threaten them with detention.

Temple reached a hand down to Dill. "You all right, son?"

Dill waved the offered hand away and stood on his own. "I'm fine. Summers here just tripped me, that's all."

"Whatever happened, it's done now, hear? Shake hands with each other and let's hope you don't cross my path between now and when I hand you your diplomas next Friday."

"Sure thing, Mr. Temple. Sorry," Ned said. He smiled and winked at Dill. "See you around, Dilly-boy."

Dill didn't reply.

Temple clapped his hands. "Good. Off you go now." He made a shooing gesture at both of them.

Ned jogged to his bike and jumped on, pedaling his way home. He had done his best to live his last life without solving this mystery, but it ate at him. It slowly wormed its way back into his consciousness until it couldn't be ignored.

Now, having made the decision and returning to the actual scene of the crime, he felt lighter than he had since that day he went out with Mary Malone that very first night. He was a one-hundred-year-old man in an eighteen-year-old's body, and yet, he felt strong and ready to take on the world.

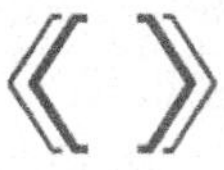

NED HAD ANOTHER EMOTIONAL reunion with his father, although William didn't understand. He never did. William had just seen Ned that morning before school, and so he couldn't figure out why Ned hugged him so tightly when he came through the door.

"I love you, Dad," Ned said.

"I love you too, Neddy. Everything okay in your world?"

"Everything's good. Dinner's almost done. Better go wash up."

"Smells good," William said, heading for the bathroom.

Over dinner, Ned said, "Can I borrow the truck tomorrow night?"

"Sure, of course. You and Stink got some big pre-graduation party to go to or something?"

Ned put his fork down and smiled at his Dad. "You're not gonna believe this, but I have a date. I'm taking Mary Malone to the movies."

"Mary Malone? Don't recognize the name. Is she in your class, or an underclassman?"

"She actually graduated two years ago. She works at the grocery store."

"Dating an older woman? You're moving up in the world," William said. Then, he paused, remembering something. "Wait, she works at the grocery store. Does that explain why you've been doing our grocery shopping bit by bit, a little bit every day?"

"I have no idea what you're talking about," Ned said. And for a minute, he didn't. He had returned to this spot—the day before his date with Mary—often enough that it felt like home. But the events that had led up to that date had long-since faded from his memory. As he remembered back, though, he did recall that he looked for an excuse to go to the grocery store most every day, just for a chance to say hello to Mary.

"Sure, you're completely innocent. Remember, I was once a teenage boy. I haven't forgotten everything. Good for you. That's the thing with us Summers men—our charms aren't immediately obvious. Sometimes we need to be around someone a bit before they pick up on how great we are."

"I didn't think anybody was ever going to pick up on me," Ned said.

"You're young, boy. Give it time."

I've lived more than a hundred years and no one's thought I was particularly charming. How long do I have to give it?

"I'll fill the truck up with gas for you tomorrow, but you might want to leave time to wash it when I get home. It gets pretty dusty and dirty sitting out on the job sites."

"Sure will, and thanks, Dad."

"Got any homework tonight?"

"Just a little. I was thinking about getting the checkerboard out after I finish it. You up for a game?"

"If you don't mind getting a lesson in how to be a good loser, I don't mind giving it to you."

Ned hurriedly washed the dishes, pretended to do the homework that he never intended to turn in, and then grabbed the checker board out of the closet.

He let his Dad beat him two out of three.

Chapter Forty

Ned woke up on Friday morning, full of purpose. He brushed his teeth, made himself some Cream of Wheat, and got on his bike for the ride to school.

Am I setting myself up for failure again? I thought I knew the answer to everything the last two times I woke up here, but I managed to foul things up.

It was a warm summer day, and Ned looked up at the blue skies and sunshine that dappled down through the trees as he rode.

Or is that the same old negative mindset that's kept me from really being happy all these years? I'm gonna go with that.

"Hey, Summers!"

Ned didn't need to look around to see who was calling him. He slowed down and said, "Hey, Stink."

"Geez, I almost missed you this morning. You rode right past me. Not gonna wait up for your old pal Stink anymore?"

"Sorry, guess I was lost in my thoughts."

Stink cast a sideways glance at Ned. "That's something I never thought I'd hear out of you. I always thought that if you had an idea, it might die of loneliness."

Ned veered his front wheel dangerously close to Stink, but Stink managed to jump out of the way. "Gonna have to be quicker than that, Summers. Whatcha got goin' tonight? Nothin' like usual?"

"Yeah, pretty much. Well, only if you call a date with the prettiest girl in town nothin.'"

"Come here. A little closer. I need to feel your forehead. I think you might have a fever."

Ned shrugged and pedaled slowly along.

"Tell me you don't mean it. You don't really have a date, do you?"

"Sure do. Taking Mary Malone to the Pickwick tonight to see *The Quiet Man.*"

Stink looked at Ned through narrowed eyes. "Now I know you're having me on. Mary Malone? She's not just out of our league. She lives in a different universe."

When Ned didn't say anything, Stink said, "Jesus, you're serious. You got a date with Mary Malone." He took a vicious kick at a rock in his path, sending it flying. He looked for something else to kick but didn't find anything. Finally, he shrugged, and said, "Well, good for us. You getting a date with a girl like that is probably the closest I'll ever come to having it happen to me."

"You should just try asking them out. Pretty girls, I mean. That's all I did. Well, after a month of buying groceries a little bit at a time to work up my nerve, that is," Ned explained.

Stink mimed a machine gunner shooting a thousand rounds into the sky, followed by a plane spiraling toward the ground. "Shot down in flames. It'll never work for me. That only works for good lookin' guys." He paused for effect. "And you, apparently."

"See ya, Stink," Ned said, veering off for the bike rack. In his last trip through life, Ned and Stink had stayed friends after graduation, but with time, they had drifted away. Despite his protests, Stink did eventually get not only a date, but a girlfriend, who eventually became his wife. They had two kids, and as Ned stayed single, Stink and Mrs. Stink had hung around more and more with other families.

I'll see if I can change that a little bit this time, too.

Ned skated through school and even paid attention to what the teachers were talking about. When he listened attentively, he found that several of them even had interesting things to say.

That night, he made meatloaf and mashed potatoes for himself and his dad.

When William walked through the door, smelled the meatloaf, and saw the mashed potatoes already on the table, he said, "What's this? Thanksgiving? I'll wash up, and then we can dig in."

When he sat down at the table, William said, "If this is the way you're going to be when you have a date, I will encourage you to ask more girls out."

Ned bolted through his dinner, much to William's amusement, and then he hustled outside to wash the Dodge.

When he opened the driver's door to let it air out, the familiar aroma of a Little Tree air freshener filled his nostrils.

That's right. Dad bought one of these the first time I took Mary out, but didn't the second time. I wonder what it is that causes some things to happen over and over, just the same, and others to be inconsistent.

He left the house a few minutes early. Didn't want to risk being late and being turned away at the door by Mrs. Malone.

He went through the same pre-date routine he had twice already by chatting up Mrs. Malone, speaking to Mr. Malone behind his newspaper, and doing his best to be charming—a skill that never came easily to Ned.

On the way to the truck, Mary tucked her arm through Ned's and said, "You handled that well. I'm impressed."

"I'm not just some kid, you know," Ned said, opening up the passenger door, and then closing it behind her.

"I'll bet you like Maureen O'Hara, don't you?" Ned asked.

"Well, who doesn't? I've been looking forward to seeing this ever since I saw some pictures of it in one of my magazines."

"How about John Wayne? What do you think of him?"

Mary wrinkled her nose a bit. "He's a good actor, but he's kind of old."

"Don't go for older men, huh?"

Mary's head snapped to the left, but Ned was just staring ahead at the road.

"Depends on the man, I suppose. Tonight, I think I like a younger man."

"I know I appear young, but I feel so much older."

For the third time, they bought their tickets. Ned bought Mary a small Coke and a Baby Ruth—another of those things that never seemed to change—and they watched *The Quiet Man.*

Coming out of the theater, Ned asked, "Still think John Wayne was too old for her?"

Mary twitched her right cheek and frowned as she thought about that. "He's handsome, but yes, I still think he's too old for her."

"Good to know. How does a chocolate shake from Artie's sound?"

"Like heaven."

They drove out to the small, shack version of Artie's, and that was another one of those things that surprised Ned, somehow. In his last trip through life, he had eaten at Artie's often—one of the hazards of being a bachelor included eating out too much—and Artie's was always good.

Ned ordered their shakes and they drank them in Artie's parking lot. He watched Mary out of the corner of his eye. She seemed blithe and unconcerned, not showing any sign that she was marked for death within a few hours.

Chapter Forty-One

After they finished their shake, Ned drove them home. He pulled up in front of the Malone family's one-story house. The porch light, naturally, was on. Somewhere behind the curtains, Ned knew that Mrs. Malone was standing watch.

"Thanks for going with me," Ned said.

I never get tired of seeing that movie.

"I had a good time," Mary said. There was a note of surprise in her voice, as though she hadn't really expected to have fun that night.

I wonder why you came then? Was it just because I asked and you didn't say no?

Ned nodded toward the picture window. "Why do I have a feeling your mom is in there right now, watching us?"

"Because you're a smart boy!" Mary sighed. "And I should go in, or else she'll give me the whole 'Mary, nice girls don't sit in parked cars with boys' spiel," she said, with a pretty fair imitation of her mother. She leaned toward Ned, all gentle perfume and soft lips.

Ned didn't turn away, but he didn't kiss her full-on, either. He turned his head slightly at the last minute, so only the corner of their mouths met for a moment.

Mary jumped back a little bit. She was not used to having young men turn away from her.

Sorry. I may look eighteen, but I'm really old enough to be your great-grandfather. Just doesn't seem right.

"Well," Mary said, a little put out, but also a little bit intrigued, "I guess I'll go in now."

"Thanks a lot, Mary. I had a swell time."

That's how we talked in 1952, right? Swell? The older I get, the harder it gets to remember everything.

Ned jumped out of the truck, hustled around it, and opened the door for her with a small bow.

Mary dimpled prettily at him, and then moved up the walk with a sensuous swing in her step. As old as he was, Ned watched her walk.

Watching a pretty girl walk never gets old, I suppose, even if I do.

Ned climbed back into the Dodge, turned the key, and ran through his plan in his mind. He drove ahead a few blocks, until he came to the intersection at Main Street, where he turned left. He puttered up Middle Falls' main drag, slowing to look inside Marv's diner, but there was just a young couple seated at a table. It would be a while before Deakins stopped in for his pie and coffee, which was just the way Ned wanted it.

He figured he had about two hours to get into position, but he wasn't going to take any chances by jumping in at the last minute.

Ned drove south out of town, then turned west onto the familiar Forest Service Road. When he had traveled this road to Deakins' cabin in his last life, he had been face down in the back of a cop car.

During his last life, Ned had tried to tell himself he didn't need to solve the mystery of Mary's murder after all. He gave lie to that idea though, by traveling back to the Deakins' cabin many times. He knew exactly how far off the highway the spur road was, and he had picked a spot a little further on where he could safely park the Dodge.

There was a small wooden bridge that ran over an offshoot of the river. Ned drove across it and found what he was looking for—a small parking lot where people could park and hike.

He turned the noisy engine off and opened his door. For a full minute, he just sat there and absorbed the quiet. William had put an air freshener in the truck that supposedly smelled like pine trees. With a small breeze rustling through actual fir and pine trees, Ned knew it was a poor substitute for what nature provided.

He slipped the truck keys into the front pocket of his jeans, then grabbed his jacket and slipped it on. It felt comfortingly heavy, with the flashlight in one pocket and the .22 in the other.

He set out on the half-mile walk back to Deakins' cabin. The moonlight made for an easy walk, and he kept the flashlight in his pocket.

Over the course of three lifetimes, Ned had given a lot of thought as to who the killer would be. He didn't have much of a clue during his first life, so he had bought into the idea of a passing drifter. When he saw Deakins drop the body in Whitaker Park, he had been sure it was him.

But then Ned had provided his own inadvertent alibi for the chief by going on the most unofficial ride-along ever. Now, with another lifetime to absorb everything he knew, he thought he had found the answer. In less than two hours, he would know whether he was right or not.

He found the spur road with no trouble and walked down the more primitive road to the cabin. The road ended in a roughed-out yard, which was where Deakins had parked his squad car in his previous life. There was a bit of a clearing around the yard, both ahead and to the left, and there was nothing but thick woods beyond it. To the right was the cabin. There was a small path that could have been a continuation of the road, but it was mostly overgrown with grass and ferns.

The cabin itself wasn't much, but the same could have been said about William and Ned's cabin before they fixed it up. The Deakins' place was typical of the hunting cabins in the area—perfectly fine for a place to sleep during hunting season, not to mention romantic trysts when you were a cheating husband.

Ned walked to the window of the cabin and shined his flashlight inside. Very typical. There was a bed, a kitchen, and a rough-hewn dining room table with an oil lamp sitting on it.

Ned turned the flashlight off and slipped it back into his pocket. He walked to the edge of the forest where he had seen Mary's body. He glanced around and found a sturdy cedar tree with a broad base. He slipped around behind it and found it offered a perfect viewpoint. He could see the cabin, as well as the spot where Deakins would pull in, and he was close enough to be able to hear what was being said.

Ned stuck his hands in his pocket, one gripping the flashlight, the other the .22.

And now, I wait.

Chapter Forty-Two

Occasionally, Ned would adjust the flashlight beam on his watch, trying to estimate how much longer it would be before Deakins showed up. Ten-thirty passed. Then, it was ten-fifty-two. In no time at all, the clock struck eleven.

He didn't expect Deakins to show up until after midnight, but if he was correct about who the killer was, he knew they would be along before then.

His patience and planning paid off a little after eleven-thirty. He heard a car coming down Forest Service Road and knew it was too early for it to be Deakins. Ned estimated that Deakins was just finishing up his pie and coffee at Marv's.

The headlights turned down the long driveway and illuminated the forest around Ned. He turned sideways and moved further behind the cedar tree.

After everything it took for me to be standing here, I don't want to be discovered right now.

The car turned right on the far side of the cabin and drove along the path Ned had seen earlier. He heard the engine turn off and saw the headlights go dim.

Ned heard footsteps come around the cabin and peeked cautiously around the cedar tree. He saw a shadowy form approach the cabin door, but he couldn't make out who it was.

Whoever they were, they pushed the cabin door open with a shove and disappeared inside. A moment later, the door slammed shut.

Ned felt comfortably out of view and stepped around the tree to look inside, expecting the lamp on the table to be lit. Instead, the interior of the cabin stayed completely dark.

I could walk over and push on that door and end this mystery, once and for all. But what good would that do? It might delay things here, but would it really stop the murder? Or would there just be one more body for Deakins to dump at Whitaker Park?

Ned waited for many long minutes, all the while keeping a vigilant watch on the cabin. Inside, there was no sign of life whatsoever—no movement, no flare of a match, and no illumination from a flashlight. Just darkness.

Finally, there was the sound of another car approaching down Forest Service Road. Once again, headlights turned down the road to Deakins' cabin.

The black and white Ford police cruiser rolled to a stop in front of the cabin. Ned glanced from the cruiser—at which point he saw two people clearly visible in the front seat—to the darkened cabin.

Why did whoever is in there wait until Deakins left? Why not come out with guns blazing right now?

It gave Ned an odd sense of déjà vu to see the scene from his current perspective behind the tree. He had a clear memory of the conversation going on in the car—Deakins trying to get Mary to go in the cabin, Mary trying to shed Deakins from her life permanently.

Didn't know it at the time, but Chief Deakins is probably fortunate he and Mary didn't go inside the cabin. I've got a hunch that wouldn't have gone too well for him.

Ned watched the two of them in the front seat. It was easy to read the body language from where he was. Mary was clearly up against the door, while Deakins had his right arm slung over the backseat, moving in close. He scooted over even farther yet and embraced her, but Ned sensed Mary was struggling against him and finally pushed him away.

Even from where he stood, Ned could tell the conversation grew heated and then Mary threw the car door open and jumped out. She left the door open behind her and took a few steps into the clearing. Then she stopped, as if she had no idea where she should go from there.

Ned glanced at the window of the cabin and saw what he hadn't seen while he was hiding face down in the squad car. A dark figure was lurking.

Deakins climbed out of the car and went over to Mary. He had left the engine running and the lights were still on, so they were lit like a dramatic silhouette—if it was a painting, it would have been called *No longer lovers,* or *Please get back in the car.*

Deakins grabbed her by the shoulders. "Mary! Mary, calm down!"

That exhortation worked as well as it ever did with any woman. She started to cry even harder. Deakins took two steps toward the cabin door and Ned held his breath.

Things can always turn out differently. If he actually goes inside, what do I do then?

Deakins didn't go inside, though. Instead, he just said, "Come inside and we can talk about it. I've got a fire all ready to go. Let's light a fire and talk. We can figure this out. I won't lose you."

Mary shook her head. "You don't get it. You've already lost me."

"Gah," Deakins said and turned away in disgust.

As soon as he did, Mary turned and ran down a path into the woods. Over her shoulder, she shouted, "Just go away! Leave me alone!"

"You're ten miles away from home. I'm not going to leave you out here!"

For a moment, Ned wished that Deakins would go into the cabin instead of driving away. He didn't. Instead, he cupped his hands around his mouth and shouted even louder than before. "Mary! Goddamn it! Come back. At least let me give you a ride home." He waited for a few seconds, and then he made a snap decision.

Loudly, in the direction Mary had disappeared, he said, "You want to walk home? Fine! Try explaining *that* to your mother!" He turned and kicked the passenger door shut, then got into the squad car. He sat there for sixty more seconds, waiting to see if Mary was going to reappear.

When she didn't, he threw his arm over the seat and quickly reversed down the driveway and onto the main road. The sound of the squad car slowly faded away to nothingness. The denizens of the forest—owls, crickets, frogs—didn't immediately start their chorus, though. People were still too close.

It's like I've been watching a movie I've already seen, but I missed the ending.

As soon as it was obvious that Deakins was gone, Mary emerged from the woods. She walked into the clearing and looked around, as though just realizing what kind of a dilemma she was in.

The door of the cabin opened inward with a loud squeal.

Mary jumped back, frightened by the unexpected noise.

Sandy Deakins stepped out of the shadows. In her shaking hand was a .22 pistol.

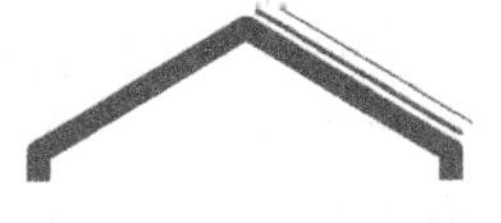

Chapter Forty-Three

Mary Malone blanched and retreated a few steps. It was impossible to tell if it was because she was so obviously caught in her affair, or if she saw the gun in Sandy Deakins' hand. Mary's own hand flew first to her throat, then to her mouth. Her ruined mascara, already running in black rivers, was spread even further by new tears.

"You're a pretty girl," Sandy said, a note of resignation in her voice. "He's always liked them pretty."

"Mrs. Deakins. Sandy," Mary said, but she could find nothing more to add. It's more difficult to find justification for an affair when looking down the working end of a pistol held by the wronged wife.

"So, you do know my name. You *do* know that I exist."

Mary nodded. "Yes." The word came out with a definite bend and quaver. "I'm sorry—"

"—Sorry?" Sandy interrupted. "Of course you're sorry. You're caught now."

"No. Honestly, I've been torn up about this for months." Mary stopped, possibly contemplating whether it was a good idea to say how long she'd been sleeping with a pregnant woman's husband while the pregnant woman held a gun. "I—I broke it off with him tonight. I tried to do it before, but I wasn't strong enough. Please believe me."

"Of course I believe you. I heard your whole sordid little story play out just now. That doesn't do anything to make up for all the times that occurred before tonight, does it?" Slowly, Sandy Deakins walked toward Mary, who seemed frozen in place. There was no doubt that Mary saw the gun now.

"I came here tonight to kill *him*, not you. But now he's gone, and you're here."

Mary wailed. It was a small, childish sound of fear coming from a grown woman.

"If I killed you with Michael's own gun, do you think they could trace it back to him? I don't know much about guns and police work, as he constantly reminds me." Sandy let the gun waver, then fall to her side. "Ah, who am I trying to kid? I can't kill you. I could kill Michael, because of everything he's done to me, but you're just another girl in a long line of girls."

Ned glanced at Mary and saw that this latest volley was obviously news to her.

I don't understand. Mary was alive when Deakins and I left, but shot dead when we came back ten minutes later. It must be that something is about to happen. An accident of some sort. The kind that happens when adrenaline, anger, and guns are mixed together. If I wait instead of trying stop it now, it'll be too late. I need to do it now.

Ned stepped out from behind the tree, his hands raised.

Mary turned, her eyes wide with shock.

Sandy turned toward Ned and her finger tightened on the trigger. The gun fired.

The bullet whizzed just over Ned's head, causing him to drop to his knees.

"Whoa, whoa, *whoa*! Ma'am, I'm not here to hurt you. I want to *help* you."

Sandy Deakins threw the gun away like it had suddenly morphed into a snake. "Sorry, sorry! I didn't mean to do that."

Ned climbed to his feet and stepped forward, holding his hands out in front of him. "It's okay. I just knew we were about to have an accident here, and I wanted to stop it from happening."

Mary squinted at Ned. "What are you doing here? I really, truly do not understand."

"And I don't think there's anything I could tell you that would help you to understand. I'm sorry. But if I hadn't been here, I believe that accidental gunshot would have hit you instead of killing a few pine cones behind me."

"How— I—" Mary shut her mouth, unable to finish a sentence.

Ned held up his finger. "Listen."

It was the sound of an approaching engine.

"That's Chief Deakins. He's coming back because he got a guilty conscience about leaving you here."

Now both Mary and Sandy looked at Ned.

"How in the world do you know?" Sandy asked.

"I told you—I can't answer that. You wouldn't believe the truth if I did. I think we all need to just relax and calm down a little before someone gets hurt."

Headlights turned down the main road. Ned took a few steps out into the clearing. While Ned and Mary looked at the oncoming lights, Sandy reached down and retrieved the gun.

The Middle Falls police car came to a sudden stop. Ned could see Deakins sitting behind the wheel, trying to make sense of the scene that was in front of him.

He opened the door slowly and stepped out. He looked from Sandy, who was holding the pistol, to Mary, and then from Mary to Ned.

The first part of that equation was easy for him to figure out. Sandy had obviously found out he was meeting Mary here at the cabin and she had come to put a stop to it. The young man in the midst of it was harder to figure.

Deakins stared at Ned, trying to place him. Finally, he asked, "Who is this guy?"

That's right. Of course. I'm back at the beginning. Deakins doesn't have any idea who I am yet.

"That's Ned Summers," Mary said quietly. "I have no idea why he's here."

"It doesn't matter why he's here, Michael," Sandy said. "That's not the point. The only thing that matters is that you've done it again, haven't you?"

Ned slipped his hand into his pocket and gripped the barrel of his pistol.

This all feels so fluid, like anything could happen, but no matter what, someone is going to die.

Michael Deakins approached his wife empty-handed. His gun belt hung on his hip, but he didn't touch it. "Honey, listen. Let's go home and talk about this. We can figure it all out. I made a mistake, and I'm sorry. I've got a problem. But you know I love you. I want to make a home for you and me and the baby. We can still do that."

"That's the way it's been before, but not this time. This is the last time."

Deakins continued to walk toward his wife. His expression was non-threatening. A slight smile even touched his lips. When he was just a few feet away, he slapped his hand out, lightning-quick. He hit Sandy's hand that held the gun, but she had gripped it tight. He knocked the barrel away to her right.

Sandy fought to hold onto the gun and, in doing so, she squeezed the trigger.

A single bullet flew through the night.

Chapter Forty-Four

The stray shot flew straight and true, missing Ned Summers and striking Mary Malone dead center. It pierced her heart and she crumpled, dead before she even hit the ground.

The crack of the gun caused Ned's finger to tighten on his own gun and that bullet, which could have easily gone high and wide, instead struck Sandy Deakins in the throat. She didn't die instantly, as Mary had, but she did fall to her knees, eyes wide, clutching at the small hole in her throat. Her clasping hands did very little to staunch the flow of blood.

Michael Deakins leaped forward and caught Sandy before she could fall all the way to the ground. He moved her hand away so he could see how bad the bleeding was. As he did, the pumping of the blood slowed until it suddenly stopped. Sandy Deakins' eyes glazed over.

Michael Deakins laid her on the ground and then he stood up quickly.

Ned looked at the gun in his hand and dropped it with a "Gah!" The impact of what he had just done sank in almost immediately.

Next, the impact of Deakins fist sent Ned sprawling.

"Who *are* you?" Deakins asked, pulling his service revolver from its holster. "And why did you just kill my wife? It's not going to change what happens to you—I'm still going to kill you. I just don't understand what you're doing here."

Deakins leveled the gun with Ned's face. He looked from Mary's body to Sandy's. "Do you see what you've done here?"

"It was an accident. I didn't mean to shoot your wife. The gun just went off."

Deakins gun did not waver. There was no shake in his hand.

"I guess I believe you."

He shrugged. Then he pulled the trigger.

Chapter Forty-Five

Ned Summers opened his eyes with a gasp. He seemed mesmerized and didn't even attempt to duck the roundhouse punch from Stanley Dill. Dill's fist hit Ned right between the eyes and he went down, flat on his back.

Dill stood over him. "Come on. Get up. Get up! I've got more of that for you."

Ned's eyes were open, but he couldn't focus. Tears leaked out of his eyes and ran behind his ears.

"Oh man, Dill, look—you made him cry!"

Ned didn't care about being punched, about being mocked, or about anything, really. He had failed. Again. He just wanted to lay on the grass and wait for the world to start making sense.

Dill stepped forward and straddled Ned. "Is that it, then? That's all you've got? One punch and you go down and stay down?"

Dill was abruptly pulled back by the strong hand of Mr. Temple. "Knock it off, Mr. Dill. I'm sure this is a triumphant moment for you, but it is done now." Temple looked around at the other boys. "Don't you all have somewhere else to be? Do you need me to find something to occupy your time?"

The crowd evaporated. Dill tried to go with it, but Temple grabbed him by the shoulder. "Not so fast. You stay right here while I assess what's going on."

Temple leaned down and stared into Ned's face. "You all right, son?"

"No, I'm not all right. Not at all."

Temple took in the flushed skin, the tears still leaking down Ned's face, and the fact that Ned seemed to have no interest in getting up. He turned to Dill. "I may need to get him to the hospital. You can go, but tell your father to expect a call from me tonight."

The triumphant look on Dill's face faded. His shoulders slumped as he turned and walked away.

"You lay still, son. Are you hurt anywhere?"

Everywhere. I'm caught in an infernal loop that I can't get out of. I know a girl is going to be murdered tomorrow night and apparently there isn't anything I can do to stop it.

"No, I'm fine. Dill didn't hit me that hard. Please don't call his dad. We were just fooling around and I slipped."

"It didn't look like you slipped. As I came up, it looked like he socked you pretty good."

"I'd like to just go home, if I could."

"Sit up first, and see how you feel."

Ned sat up, and then he stood up. He wiped his face with his T-shirt, then said, "Honestly, Mr. Temple, I'm fine."

Temple put a heavy hand on his shoulder and looked into Ned's eyes. After a moment, he patted his shoulder and said, "All right. That's fine, then. If you and Mr. Dill have a score to settle, why don't you wait until after graduation, when you will be the problem of the Middle Falls police department, instead of Middle Falls High School?"

"Yes, sir. Thank you, sir."

Ned trudged to the bicycle rack and pulled his bike out. He didn't jump on and ride, though. He just pushed it along.

So, what's next? Home to make dinner for Dad again? Go out with Mary tomorrow night, then try to save her but just fail instead? I can't do it. I'm spiritually exhausted. I could go home, lay down on my bed, and sleep for a lifetime. Except, if I do, I'll eventually starve to death and wake up getting punched by Dill again.

Involuntarily, his hand went to the nexus point between his eyes, which was red and swollen.

Eventually, he swung his leg over the seat and pumped the pedals slowly. He didn't head home. As much as he loved his dad, Ned was not ready to fall back into the same routine as he so often had done.

He didn't pay attention to where he was going, but when he looked up, he saw he was at Whitaker Park.

"Of course," he mumbled to himself. "Why not?"

He turned his bike down the road and pedaled right by the spot he had once believed to be the location of Mary's murder. Once again, it was just a slightly overgrown spot on the edge of the park. This spot's place in the drama wouldn't begin for another day.

Ned pushed on past and rode over to the small children's playground. He dropped the bike in the grass and sat in the rubber loop of a child's swing.

So what now? I guess I could follow Sandy Deakins from her house and run her car off the road, but would that really do it? Would she just kill Mary a few days later, or would it maybe be Chief Deakins' gun that accidentally goes off at the cabin?

Laconically, he pushed off with his shoe and swung back a few inches.

Or can I just learn to let this go? To admit that I've spent these lifetimes trying to save Mary, and I just can't do it? Does letting go mean I'm giving up?

"Sometimes, giving up is the only path to peace."

Ned jumped six inches in the air. He was alone in the playground. He *knew* was alone.

He turned his head and saw a young woman beside him, smiling placidly.

Chapter Forty-Six

Ned threw himself violently out of the swing, stumbling forward and falling on his butt. He crab-walked away from her a few feet, then sat down.

She couldn't have looked less threatening. She was pretty, with long black hair, and she was dressed in flowing white robes that looked a bit like the clouds had come down from the sky and wrapped around her.

"Who—who are you?"

"The same question Chief Deakins asked you not long ago. Or, should I say, a quick lifetime ago?"

"What the hell? You know what's happening to me. I don't even have to tell you. You already *know.*"

The woman bowed her head in acknowledgement of this fact.

"I am Semolina."

"Hi. I'm Ned. How'd you do that trick where you just materialized like that?"

"How'd you do the trick where you materialized back in the school yard each time you die?"

"Point taken. So, you're an angel or something? Or, maybe a devil that is punishing me for some unknown sin?"

"Sin is surprisingly irrelevant where I work. Weights and balances tend to all work themselves out over time."

"You talk like a philosophy book."

"Do I?" She looked pleased, though Ned had not meant it as a compliment. "I always thought everyone else at the Universal Life Center spoke as if they were quoting a fortune cookie."

"Universal Life—okay, whatever. Aside from scaring me half to death, can I ask what you're doing here on this backward little planet?"

"I came to see you, of course. You're my job."

"I apologize, then. I must be quite a disappointment."

"Not at all. I came because my Pyxis showed me how discouraged you were. My training says I need to disassociate myself from results, but I haven't mastered that yet. When someone I watch over is discouraged, I feel the need to help, at least as much as I can."

"I feel like I've been running in the same stupid circle over and over again, life after life."

"I agree, you have."

"If you came to make me feel better, you've got a strange way of accomplishing it."

"I prefer speaking the truth to simply making someone feel better. I will always tell you the truth."

"What did you mean when you first said that giving up is the only path to peace?"

"Let me tell you a story."

"That's the way these things always work, isn't it? No straight answer. Just a story, and I'm supposed to figure out the moral." Ned stood up and dusted himself up, then sat back down in the swing.

"When I first transitioned from life to after-life, I was trained to be a Watcher. As part of my training, I was given a manual. It was very confusing. Sometimes the book could read my thoughts, sometimes it was just frustrating. There was another person in my class named Carrie. We both struggled with this frustrating book. After a time, Carrie slammed the book shut and said, 'I give up.'"

Semolina looked sideways at Ned, who had turned in the swing and was watching her intently.

"Poof! Just like that, Carrie disappeared. I thought she'd been punished for giving up. It wasn't until much, much later that I, myself, gave up. That was when I graduated. We had to learn that we can't fix everything. When we gave up, we moved on."

Semolina pushed off and gave a mighty swing. "Woooh!" she said. "We don't have anything this fun at the Universal Life Center."

"So that's the answer then? Just give up?"

"I would never say that's *the* answer. It's *an* answer. Do you know what prescriptivism is?'

"I barely graduated high school, then spent fifty years living in a cabin. Oh wait. You know that already. So, no, I have no idea what that is."

"It's the idea that there's *one way* to do something. As in *you must* do X, Y, or Z."

"Oh, sure."

"In the Universal Life Center, we're not big on that idea. There is more than one way to climb a mountain. Once you're where you want to be, it doesn't matter which method you used to get there."

"Unless the method I choose hurts someone else."

Semolina continued to swing, but she didn't say anything.

Finally, she said, "We believe in self-determination and free choice. You are completely free to choose whatever path you want for this life and whatever life may lay beyond."

"Will you answer a question for me?"

"Possibly."

"Can I stop Mary from being killed?"

"Why ask me a question you already know the answer to?"

"You were right. It is like asking a question of a fortune cookie."

"Here's a fortune cookie someone wise once had: 'Know that you are safe. That you are loved. That you are perfect. That no harm can ever come to you.'"

"I don't feel very perfect," Ned said. He turned to look at Semolina.

She was gone.

Chapter Forty-Seven

Ned pushed off with the toe of his tennis shoe and the swing gained momentum.

So I'm not crazy. There's this whole system that has been picking me up and dropping me back in the same place over and over. Or else, I'm so crazy that I just imagined this Semolina person. I don't think so, though. I never would have made up a name like that.

At the peak of the swing's arc, Ned jumped off, landing neatly. He took a small bow for the imaginary audience.

The question is why? Why am I continually being dropped back to this particular spot? What do I need to learn? Figuring out the mystery of who actually killed Mary wasn't it. It's got to be something about me, not things outside myself.

Ned walked through the park, hands in his pockets, focusing his attention inward.

I think I need to worry more about myself. Mary put herself in that horrible position. She didn't deserve to be shot for it, but I don't think I should be butting in where I don't belong. That's a situation between Mary, Sandy, and Michael Deakins. I think maybe I've been trying to inject myself into a situation I just wasn't intended to be a part of.

Ned returned to his bike and headed home.

Even in my first life, before all this craziness started, I was only involved on the periphery. I ran to the cabin and stayed there because I wanted to. When I came back to town, no one pointed fingers or talked about me. I just wanted to be isolated. I've always been isolated. It's become a habit to wall myself off from the rest of the world.

Ned pulled his bike into the driveway at the same moment his dad arrived. He dropped his bike in the grass and said, "Sorry. Got caught up in something after school, so dinner's not ready."

William dismissed that idea with a gesture. "Don't worry about it. You don't have to make dinner every night, you know. Come on, I'll get washed up and help you out."

Forty-five minutes later, the two of them sat at the table, eating quietly.

One thing's for sure. I don't want to be the number one suspect in Mary's murder again. That was no fun.

"Hey, Dad? Would it be okay if I had a few of the guys over for a card game tomorrow?"

"What kind of cards?"

"I thought we might play a little penny poker."

"All that money from the hardware store burning a hole in your pocket, huh?"

"I just know that graduation's coming up next week, so I thought maybe I'd hang out with the guys while I still can."

"Sure, if you can keep it down to a dull roar after I go to bed."

"You bet," Ned said with a smile. He realized he was actually looking forward to that. "I kind of had a date for tomorrow, but I think I'm going to cancel that and just have the guys over instead."

"It's your life, son, and you've got plenty of time to live it. There's lots of time ahead for girls and dates."

'Plenty of time to live it,' huh? Right you are, Dad.

"Go ahead and read your paper. I've got the dishes."

Ned hurried as he cleaned up, and then, he made the worst phone call first. Picking up the heavy receiver on the wall phone, he dialed the Malones' number.

"Hello, Malone residence." It was Mary's little sister, whose name Ned still couldn't remember.

"Hi, this is Ned Summers. Is Mary there?"

"Nope."

"Can you give her a message for me? I had a date scheduled with her for tomorrow night—"

"—Join the parade," the girl chimed in.

"Uh, yeah. Anyway, I can't make it. Can you let your sister know?"

"Ned, tomorrow night, can't make it. Yeah, I can handle that."

"Thank you," Ned said, then added "'Bye," and hung up the phone. A sense of relief flooded through him.

I really am sorry, Mary, but I can't change your life.

Ned picked up the receiver again and dialed Stink's number. A woman's voice answered.

"Hello, Mrs. Mitchell. Is...uh, Vernon there?"

Shit, almost called him Stink to his mother. Not cool.

"Of course. Can I tell him who's calling?"

"It's Ned Summers."

"Oh, hello, Ned. Just a moment and I'll get him for you."

Ned heard the phone clank down on a countertop in the Mitchell kitchen. A moment later, he heard Stink's voice on the other end of the line.

"Whatcha doin', Stink?"

"Watching TV. It's Thursday, so *The Lone Ranger* is on."

"Hey, listen, I know this is kind of at the last minute, but whaddya say we have a card game tomorrow night?"

"I heard you got your clock cleaned by Dilly after school today."

"Yep, no doubt, but whaddya say to a card game tomorrow?"

"I don't know. Maybe."

"C'mon, what, do you have a hot date tomorrow?"

"Pretty sure you know the answer to that, and don't be evil. I'm kinda broke, though."

"We'll just play for pennies, and I'll front you to get you started. I'll grab us some Cokes at the store, too."

"Yeah, okay. Who else?"

"How about Mike and Neil? You call Mike, I'll call Neil."

"Okay. It's a safe bet they don't have anything going either."

"Why don't you come by around seven?"

Ten minutes later, Ned had called Neil Powell and the game was set.

Let's see anybody try to challenge that *alibi. Home with my dad and three friends all night.*

Chapter Forty-Eight

The poker game got off to a slightly awkward start. The four boys had been friends since elementary school, but once high school arrived, they had drifted apart.

Ned, who was usually the most reserved, opened the door and did his best to put them at ease. He laughed with them and poked fun at himself, which is always a winning strategy in these situations.

By seven-thirty, when Ned knew that *The Quiet Man* was playing at the Pickwick, the cards were in the air and there were pennies in the middle of the table.

Ned had gone to the bank as soon as school was out, and he had withdrawn five dollars from his savings account, asking for it in rolls of pennies. He surprised Stink, Mike, and Neil with two rolls of pennies each, so everyone had plenty to play with.

William also had a surprise up his sleeve. While the boys started the game, he drove to Artie's and bought hamburgers and fries for everyone.

It was an unparalleled splurge in a household known for thriftiness.

As the evening progressed, Ned couldn't help but keep an eye on the clock, all the while knowing that the drama at the cabin was drawing closer.

At nine, William asked if he could be dealt in for a few hands. The boys all scooted around the table and made room for him. He played for an hour and didn't win a single hand. The other boys were more than happy to have his pennies circulating in the game.

At ten, William excused himself, saying he had to go to bed before he ended up having to take out a second mortgage on the house to pay his gambling debts.

At eleven, Stink asked if it was okay for them to keep playing, since Mr. Summers was asleep. Ned told them his dad slept soundly, so they kept playing. Between hands, Ned watched the clock's hands go around and around, the whole time picturing what was happening out on Forest Service Road.

At midnight, Mike's father pulled up outside to take him home. He offered to give Neil a ride home at the same time. That left only two players in the game, which effectively ended it.

Stink had told his parents he was going to sleep over, so he and Ned got the sleeping bags down from the closet and laid them out in the living room. While he was in the closet, Ned also got the checkerboard down. He and Stink laid in the bags on the floor and played checkers for an hour. Eventually, Stink fell asleep in between moves.

Ned put the men and the board away. He laid down in his bag and crossed his hands under his head.

It's done. The die is cast. I'm sorry, Mary.

NED GOT UP THE NEXT day and walked Stink home before heading off to his day of stacking lumber at Coppen's Hardware.

As much as he tried to just live his life, the weekend weighed heavily on him. He went straight home after work and spent the evening with his dad. He resisted the urge to ride by Whitaker Park.

On Sunday, he decided to mow the dirt patch out in front of the house, knowing that Deakins would be by to talk with him.

When the Middle Falls squad car pulled up in front of his house, Ned turned off the mower and did his best to be polite to the man who had shot him in the face just a few days earlier.

"Are you Ned Summers?" Deakins asked, looking at the house number alongside the front door.

I'll never get used to having to meet him again over and over. I hope I don't have to do this ever again after this.

"Yes. What can I do for you?"

"Oh, nothing much. I'm just looking into a missing person call we had this morning for a young woman named Mary Malone. When I spoke to her mother this morning, she said that you had a date with her last night, but that you canceled it. Is that right?"

"Yeah. I had asked her out a week ago, because I heard her say she was breaking up with her boyfriend, who was a real jerk."

Deakins, who had been jotting something down in a small notebook, looked up suddenly. He fixed Ned with a piercing gaze.

That's the same expression you had just before you shot me, asshole.

"Did she say anything about that? Maybe who he was? I'll want to follow up with him."

"No, she didn't say who he was."

Deakins visibly relaxed.

"She just said he was an older guy with bad breath and body odor, and that she was tired of it."

"Uh-huh. Seems like an odd thing for her to say."

"I dunno. Anyway, I kind of asked her out on a lark, but I didn't really have enough money to take her anywhere, so I called and talked to her little sister on Thursday. I left a message for her, saying that I wouldn't be able to go on the date with Mary."

Deakins flipped through his notebook. Ned noticed that his jaw was set in a very firm line.

"That matches what Mrs. Malone told me." He flipped through a few more pages, looking at his notes. "I guess that's all I need from you. Thanks."

Deakins turned and pulled away from the Summers house a little faster than he needed to.

Chapter Forty-Nine

Ned Summer's fifth life was different in every way in comparison to his previous four. He didn't live as a hermit in the woods, or as a prisoner, or as an isolated man surrounded by neighbors despite feeling all alone.

He also didn't take his father up on the offer for an apprenticeship with the union. He had lived that life once, and although that work was fine, it wasn't fulfilling for him.

Those were the things he *didn't* do. What's more important, of course, is what he *did* do.

The first thing was that he didn't remain a "dateless wonder"—as Stink had dubbed him—for very long. He changed his mind about schooling and went to Middle Falls Community College for two years. While there, he met Amelie, a fetching red-haired young woman who took a fancy to him.

They dated for a few years while Ned continued to live at home with William. By late spring of 1954, Amelie graduated and was certified as a registered nurse. Ned also graduated with an Associate's degree, but he knew he needed a four-year degree to get the job he wanted, so he applied to—and was accepted at—The University of Oregon.

Both he and Amelie knew that they would be miserable without each other if he moved to the U of O alone, so Ned found a solution. He asked Amelie to marry him. She happily agreed and they held a quiet wedding at Amelie's parents' house in July. Stink served as Ned's best man.

Before he left to finish his degree, Ned had another piece of unfinished business he wanted to attend to. He knew that if things held true to form, his father would die in another five years. Ned couldn't picture leaving him alone for most of those years while he finished school.

He found the phone number for Nancy Sturgis, the woman who had twice attended his father's funeral in previous lives. He considered playing games and trying to come up with something clever, but that had never worked well for Ned.

Instead, he simply called her, explained who he was, and invited her to dinner. It took a little persuasion, but he convinced her to come to his house for dinner with him, Amelie, and William.

Then, he swallowed hard and told William what he had done.

"I don't understand," William said. "How would you even know who Nancy is? I haven't spoken to her in twenty-five years."

Ned refused to explain, but William agreed to dinner—nothing more.

Amelie was by far the better cook between herself and Ned, so she cooked the dinner for that evening. She made her grandmother's lasagna, which took her most of the day. She questioned the wisdom of setting William up with a woman he hadn't seen in such a long time, but she had seen Ned be innately right about things he should have had no idea about before, so she held her peace.

Ned simply remembered the look he had seen in her eyes at William's funerals and he had faith.

Ned and Amelie carried the conversational load at the beginning of the meal, but by desert, William and Nancy finally allowed themselves to reminisce about a first date they had many years earlier. Amelie asked a few questions to encourage the story, then sat back and watched.

Ned simply smiled. He knew.

A month later, Ned and Amelie moved to Eugene. Amelie went to work in the local hospital. Ned returned to his studies.

In the summer of 1955, he returned to Middle Falls for William and Nancy's wedding. He stood as his father's best man. Nancy's daughter, from her husband who had also died years earlier, was her bridesmaid.

Ned worked diligently at the U of O, as he was not the most naturally talented student. In the spring of 1956, he graduated with a degree in Forestry. Ever since his first life, he had enjoyed his time in the woods. Working for the Forest Service would give him time in the deep woods while still having a home to come to with Amelie.

They relocated to Susanville, California, a lovely, small town forty miles east of Mount Lassen, which was the southernmost active volcano in the Cascade Range.

William Summers did not die in October of 1959. His death, like almost all events, was fluid and changeable. It could have been that Nancy was a healthier cook, or because of the long evening walks they took. Or, it could have been that it just wasn't his time to go in this life.

A major event did occur in Ned and Amelie's life in October of 1959, though. Their only child—a boy they chose to name William after his paternal grandfather—was born.

William, who they called Will to differentiate him from his Papa William, was a headstrong child who inherited the stubbornness of his father and carefree spirit of his mother. This made him a challenging child to raise.

A co-worker in the forestry service told Ned about an incredible school in Northern California called Hartfield Academy. After many hours of discussion and gnashing of teeth, Ned and Amelie visited the academy and spoke to Curtis Hartfield, the man who ran the school. They were so impressed with him that they agreed to let Will attend for one year, then revisit the idea thereafter.

Ten years later, Ned and Amelie, along with William and Nancy, sat under a canopy on the front lawn of Hartsfield Academy and watched Will—their stubborn, hot-headed Will—graduate as valedictorian of his class.

They hoped that Will would come back to Susanville and live somewhere near them, but instead, he chose to remain at the Academy and work with the new commander there—Michael Hollister. He still came home to see them whenever he could.

William passed away in 1978. Ned had no real idea how or why, but he had enjoyed nineteen more years with his dad in this life. His dad had been happy in his life with Nora, and he found happiness once again with Nancy.

William's death was hard on Ned. Losing a parent, even for the fifth time, is always hard.

Chapter Fifty

Ned and Amelie lived a long and happy life together. No marriage is perfect, but theirs was close. They loved, respected, and listened to each other. When they disagreed, they found a way to compromise. Most importantly, whenever something happened to one of them, they couldn't wait to tell the other.

The technological advances of the eighties, nineties, and new millennia were all new to Ned. The only time he had lived to the turn of the century previously, he had been living the life of a hermit at the end of Hairy Man Road. He enjoyed it all—VCRs, personal computers, the Internet—because it was all new to him.

Ned's anxiety increased as he neared June 17, 2004—the day he had died in his first life. He had every fear that he would die once again that day.

Ned didn't fear death at all. More than almost everyone, he had every reason to know there was something to come after this life. However, he loved this particular life.

He needn't have worried. That date came and went without so much as a cold or fever.

Ned Summers lived another six years after what he had come to think of as his own personal expiration date.

In his first life, as soon as it was obvious he was dying, he drank tea from the western water hemlock to help himself on.

In 2010, when he learned he had pancreatic cancer, he had no interest in taking the fast way out.

For one thing, he feared he would open his eyes the week before graduation, in the year 1952, with Stanley Dill taking a wild swing at him. As much as he loved the way this life turned out, he didn't want to have to try to recreate it. He was tired.

More than anything, he wanted to spend as much time as he could with Amelie and Will, as well as his daughter-in-law Lisa, and, in particular, his grand-baby, Michael.

When the time came, as it inevitably did, he was surrounded by his family. Starting with Michael, they all told Ned something special he had done for them, and why they would always remember him.

After the emotional high of that, everyone but Amelie left to get something to drink at the cafeteria. Ned asked Amelie if she would go and ask the nurse to bring him some water. He watched her leave, loving her with his whole heart, right until the end. He knew it was his time, but he couldn't bear to die in front of her. While she was gone, he let go of what he had been holding onto so tightly.

And with that, Ned Summers died.

Chapter Fifty-One

Ned Summers did not open his eyes in Middle Falls, Oregon, in 1952.

He went on.

Author's Note

This book was so much fun to write. I've read mysteries since I was a little boy—The Hardy Boys were my entry drug into that world, soon followed by *Perry Mason Mysteries*—but I've never taken a swing at writing one before.

As with most things I have attempted in my life, it was more of a challenge than I had anticipated! Will I write another mystery in the future? I think I might. I will say that I have a new respect for authors that are able to put all the pieces in plain sight—red herrings, actual clues, viable suspects by the dozen—and make it all look effortless. I don't know if I'll ever achieve that level of mastery of the form.

Before I contemplate writing another mystery, though, I've got a pretty full plate. I've already decided to write a tenth book in the *Middle Falls Time Travel Series.* It will be called *The Empathetic Life of Rebecca Wright* and it will be published in May of 2019. If you enjoy the Middle Falls books and want to make sure you have them all, I'll put a link after this note to the preorder. You can buy it now and it will magically show up on your Kindle at midnight on the day it is published.

I've also got a follow-on to *The Vigilante Life of Scott McKenzie* that will be set in the Middle Falls world, but won't be directly involved with time travel. Those will be called *Agents of Karma.* I'm looking forward to writing those, because who doesn't like to see people get exactly what they deserve?

Aside from simply being a mystery, Ned's story was a challenging one for me to write. In addition to the mystery elements, there was also the fact that Ned liked to play his cards so close to the vest—even from me. I think I used less interior monologue in this book than in any other Middle Falls book, and that was the reason. Ned often hid his thoughts even from me, his creator. Some characters are so ungrateful. I guess I did put him through a lot, though, so I understand it.

I can see it's possible that some people may be unhappy with the ending of the book. After all, Ned fought very hard to accomplish something and in the end, he had to admit that he just couldn't do it. That was my plan for this book from the very beginning, though, and I stuck with it. If you were rooting for Ned to be able to finally save Mary Malone, my apologies.

As always, so many people helped me in the creation of this book.

Linda Boulanger from TreasureLine Books made the beautiful cover. I can't imagine doing a book without her.

My ace proofreaders were once again Mark Sturgell and Debra Galvan. They catch so many of my errant typos that I hope I never have to publish without them.

I also want to give a shout-out to my Advance Readers. They get to see all my books before they are completely finished and help me identify a lot of my mistakes before they even make it to my editors and proofreaders. If you enjoy the Middle Falls books and would like to be one of my Advance Readers, join my Facebook group at https://www.facebook.com/groups/776542355757488/

Of course, I owe the most to you, my friend and reader. You are the reason I have the terrific commute that I do—from bedroom to office—every morning.

Shawn Inmon
Seaview, WA
February 2019

Rebecca Wright had an enviable life, and she enjoyed that envy. She had a beautiful house, handsome husband, and a no-limit credit card. What she didn't have was empathy.

In the world of Middle Falls, you often get several chances to find what you really need. Rebecca may need every chance she can get.

The Empathetic Life of Rebecca Wright[1] is the tenth novel in the Middle Falls Time Travel series. Like all books in the series it can be read completely as a standalone novel.

1. *https://amzn.to/2Ivx6Yi*

[2]

2. https://amzn.to/2Ivx6Yi

Other Books by Shawn Inmon

The Unusual Second Life of Thomas Weaver[1] – Book one of the Middle Falls Time Travel Series. Thomas Weaver led a wasted life, but divine intervention gives him a chance to do it all over again. What would you do, if you could do it all again?

The Redemption of Michael Hollister[2] — Book two of the Middle Falls Time Travel Series. Michael Hollister was evil in Thomas Weaver's story. Is it possible for a murderer to find true redemption?

The Death and Life of Dominick Davidner[3] – Book Three of the Middle Falls Time Travel Series. When Dominick is murdered, he awakens back in his eight year old body with one thought: how to find Emily, the love of his life.

The Final Life of Nathaniel Moon[4] – Book Four of the Middle Falls Time Travel Series. Nathaniel Moon gains perfect consciousness in the womb, but when he tries to use his miraculous powers to do good, difficulties follow.

The Emancipation of Veronica McAllister[5] – Book Five of the Middle Falls Time Travel Series. Veronica McAllister said she was no good at life. When she dies and wakes up back in 1958, though, she has a second chance.

The Changing Lives of Joe Hart[6] – Book Six of the Middle Falls Time Travel Series. Joe Hart dies in 2004, but wakes up in his eighteen year old body and decides to change the world. As always, that isn't easy.

The Vigilante Life of Scott McKenzie[7] – Book Seven of the Middle Falls Time Travel Series. Scott McKenzie is a Vietnam Vet who has a hard time adjusting to civilian life. When he overdoses and dies, he wakes up just after he was released from the VA hospital. He decides to stop crimes before they are committed.

---

1. *https://www.amazon.com/Unusual-Second-Life-Thomas-Weaver-ebook/dp/B01J8FBONO*
2. *http://amzn.to/2wyUfCH*
3. *http://amzn.to/2yTgHnk*
4. *https://www.amazon.com/gp/product/B078H3376R*
5. *http://amzn.to/2HkHegL*
6. *https://amzn.to/2rYBqVh*
7. *https://amzn.to/2LgxmLq*

Feels Like the First Time[8] – Shawn's first book, his true story of falling in love with the girl next door in the 1970's, losing her for 30 years, and miraculously finding her again. It is filled with nostalgia for a bygone era of high school dances, first love, and making out in the backseat of a Chevy Vega.

Both Sides Now[9] – It's the same true story as *Feels Like the First Time,* but told from Dawn's perspective. It will surprise no one that first love and loss feels very different to a young girl than it did for a young boy.

Rock 'n Roll Heaven[10] – Small-time guitarist Jimmy "Guitar" Velvet dies and ends up in Rock 'n Roll Heaven, where he meets Elvis Presley, Buddy Holly, Jim Morrison, and many other icons. To his great surprise, he learns that heaven might need him more than he needs it.

Second Chance Love[11] – Steve and Elizabeth were best friends in high school and college, but were separated by a family tragedy before either could confess that they were in love with the other. A chance meeting on a Christmas tree lot twenty years later gives them a second chance.

Life is Short[12] – A collection of all of Shawn's short writings. Thirteen stories, ranging from short memoirs about summers in Alaska, to the satire of obsessed fans.

A Lap Around America[13] – Shawn and Dawn quit good jobs and set out to see America. They saved you a spot in the car, so come along and visit national parks, tourist traps, and more than 13,000 miles of the back roads of America, all without leaving your easy chair.

A Lap Around Alaska[14] – Have you ever wanted to drive the Alaska Highway across Canada, then make a lap around central Alaska? Here's your chance! Includes 100 photographs!

---

8. *https://www.amazon.com/Feels-Like-First-Time-Story-ebook/dp/B00961VIIM*
9. *https://www.amazon.com/Both-Sides-Now-True-Story-ebook/dp/B00DV5GQ54*
10. *https://www.amazon.com/Rock-Roll-Heaven-Shawn-Inmon-ebook/dp/B00J9T1GQA*
11. *https://www.amazon.com/Second-Chance-Love-Shawn-Inmon-ebook/dp/B00T6MU7AQ*
12. *https://www.amazon.com/Life-Short-Collected-Fiction-Shawn-ebook/dp/B01MRCXNS3*
13. *https://www.amazon.com/Lap-Around-America-ebook/dp/B06XY9GSWC*
14. *https://www.amazon.com/Lap-Around-Alaska-AlCan-Adventure-ebook/dp/B0744CVWT4/ref=sr_1_4?s=digital-text&ie=UTF8&qid=1506966654&sr=1-4&keywords=shawn+inmon+kindle+books*

Made in United States
North Haven, CT
11 December 2023